THE GREAT REPUBLIC

A POLITICAL PHANTASY

G H MATHIESON

(George Musgrave)

ISBN-13: 978-0995586833

ISBN-10: 0995586837

Originally published in 1953

in Georgetown (British Guiana, now Guyana)

Published in 2018 in the United Kingdom

by

Lightship Guides & Publications

(lightshipguides@gmail.com)

Table of Contents

Foreword

The story you are about to read is a satire. It is a warning to a nation. A humorous but polite warning of the dangers ahead for a restless People seeking independence from a Colonial Power.

It could be any Developing Nation, trying to shake off the shackles of Imperialism.

But it is actually about the South American colony of British Guiana, seeking independence from the British.

This spoof novel was originally published in 1953 as a serial in one of the national newspapers, *The Daily Argosy*.

It was written by my father, George Musgrave. Fearing reprisals and on the advice of his editor, my father wrote the story using a pseudonym, G H Mathieson. George had been working at that time as a church minister at Smith Church, Brickdam, in the capital city of Georgetown, where he was raising a young but large family of five children. (George Mathieson was the name of his favourite hymn writer.)

In the story, El Dragon helps his people struggle free from the Imperialists. But as soon as the victorious day arrives and the Colonialists depart, the People discover their country has been drained of finance, machinery, utilities and infrastructure. Even the Armed Forces have to resort to raiding the Museums to find anything with which to maintain the peace – suits of armour, spears, Medieval pikes. You can tell they are really scraping the barrel bottom when the currency becomes a system of *Purchase Tickets* (i.o.u. promises), and the most effective form of punishment is to force miscreants to be oarsmen in the national fleet of rowing boats. The only solution is to seek help from *The Great Ally Across the Seas*. And to do that, El Dragon has to go in person, cap in hand, to beg support from the foreign power.

He may have found it difficult crossing continents. But his troubles escalate when he tries to return to his own country where poverty has become so rife, even pairs of trousers, and cups and saucers have become prized possessions, to be guarded at all costs. Unrecognised by his compatriots, El Dragon has trouble convincing anyone of his mission, and is soon held captive. But he must escape before the delegates arrive from the Great Ally...

Alas, El Dragon has a severe case of digging deeper holes when already wallowing in the mire!

The story has about it the air of the film *The Mouse That Roared*, in which a ragtag Nation full of idiocies and idiosyncrasies, try to raise their heads above the proverbial parapet. But the novel predates that film by several years.

For the main protagonist, *El Dragon*, perhaps substitute Prime Minister Cheddi Jagan. For *The Great Ally Across the Seas*, consider Russia. *Bombador* is probably Brazil, *Vascalia* (Venezuela), *Threepops* (Trinidad), and the Imperialists are obviously the British.

In writing this novel, my father was not trying to stand loyally with the Imperialists. Rather, he was questioning the desire for independence for independence sake. He was merely pointing out the need for treading carefully, and for assessing repercussions when the economic and political structures that enable a State to stand on its own two feet are not put in place. This of course should be a co-operative act in liaison with the exiting Colonial Power.

British Guiana was a humid tropical country close to the Equator. The indigenous Amerindians were a minority; the main population comprised descendants of African slaves sent to work the sugar plantations in Demarara, and a large number of East Indian immigrants. It had a large area made up of tropical rainforest, and some Savannah, and a comparatively small population.

Several years later British Guiana did gain its independence (in 1966), and was renamed Guyana, and to this day remains a member of the British Commonwealth.

Though the story satires one nation's faltering attempts, it could be applicable to any number of similar restless and aspirant territories. In fact, parallels could even be made with the UK seeking separation from the EEC.

After serialisation by *The Daily Argosy*, my father had the story compiled and stapled in booklet form. And to economise, the typeface was small and condensed minimising the number of pages, making the novel off-putting and difficult to read. This is a shame, for it is actually an entertaining tale. And so this book is my attempt to republish my father's work in a more readable format.

George Musgrave died in Eastbourne in the United Kingdom in 2012.

Andrew Musgrave, 2018

Preface

The author of *The Great Republic* has chosen the medium of satire in the hope that the reader, in addition to being amused, will consider squarely the fact that the Independence of a small country, unless it has considerable capital and equipment, is likely to prove an empty dream or even a nightmare.

We draw your attention to the fact that the story was written in August 1953.

On October 2nd a bid for Independence in British Guiana was announced.

On October 4th The Great Republic began to appear as a serial in *The Daily Argosy*.

On October 7th Troops were rushed to British Guiana.

Since then certain things have come to light which bring added poignancy to the story.

This is a story which cannot lightly be dismissed.

You will be amused by the predicament of El Dragon – but it will make you think.

George Musgrave

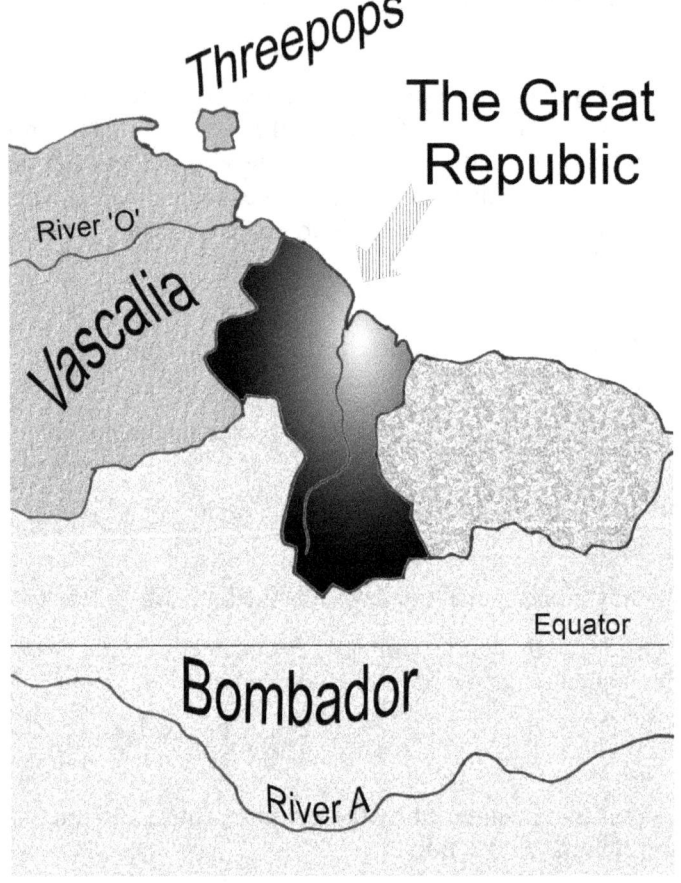

Chapter 1.

El Dragon turned restlessly in his bed. He was tired, desperately tired, but sleep would not come.

This had been the great day when the Republic had been proclaimed from the balcony of the Public Buildings. If only his wife could have been with him, to stand at his side and wave to the People!

At the thought of his wife a terrible bitterness rose within him. The irony of it that she had not remained to see this day. He tried to put the thought from his mind. He must give himself to the work in hand. He was Leader of the Republic. The People looked to him. He must work, work, work for the People.

Outside he could hear the sound of drunken revelry and now and then the crash of breaking glass. He was a little worried about it. This must not go on. But useless to try to stop the People in the height of their rejoicing. Tonight, let them have their fling. Tomorrow they must settle down to work.

His mind travelled back over the events that had led to this triumphant day. To think that in so short a time so great a change had been wrought. And El Dragon was still a young man. What a glorious future awaited the People under his leadership.

He thought of the beginnings of the Party when they had had their first dreams and plans for the liberation of an oppressed People. He recalled the little meetings in cottages and offices where they had first laid their plans. A pity that some of the original members had to go — they had been enthusiastic enough at the beginning. It was a pity there had been those differences, but with so much at stake there could only be one Leader. Fate had decreed that it should be El Dragon.

Fate! Whatever was he thinking about! That was religious nonsense which must be removed from the People. There was far too much religious sentiment about. Time and again it had frustrated their plans. He could not understand the People. They were just gullible fools, easily led, easily swept away by emotion. They must be educated. They just would not see, most of them, that religion had been one of the great weapons the Imperialist Power had used to keep them in subjection. Some of his best friends had had to go on that very issue. A pity, a great pity! It hurt him a little to think that on this great day of triumph he had not got everybody with him.

He thought about some of them, remembering their zeal of the early days, the great open air meetings when he and his key men had first put hope into the hearts of the People. Then had come the great uphill struggle against the stranglehold of the moneyed tyrants, the Foreign Capitalists, who had held the country in their power. But all that was finished now, thanks to the Party.

He thrilled at the recollection of the first great success of the Party at the election of 195— when they had been swept into power by the People. Despite all the tricks of the Capitalists they had won through. The People had spoken after the long years of heartbreak and oppression, and the People had spoken in no uncertain terms.

He thought of his wife and the great help she had been in the struggle. He wept at the recollection of her eager face and passionate utterances. She had been a dear, sweet companion. Oh God, how he heeded her now. But perhaps she was very close to him.

He turned angrily in his bed. Enough of that. There he was, drifting into religious sentiment again — that was one thing that he was not going to tolerate in himself or anyone else. That sort of nonsense must stop.

A clock struck two. He turned again somewhat irritably. He needed sleep badly but sleep would not come. He was tired, desperately tired, but it was not the tiredness of a busy day, it was the weariness from the strain of the long campaign. He had not realised until now what those years had cost him. The elation of the Great Day had freshened him for a few hours but now he was aware of a great weariness and the desire for sleep which would not come.

It had been a bitter struggle after that memorable election. The opposition had been more difficult than he had expected, the problems greater than he had imagined. The People had become impatient because promises had not been quickly fulfilled. The People just had not understood that you cannot eliminate a regime overnight. The roots of the old system were so deep, the power of money so great, the restrictions of the Imperialist Power so sinister.

Progress had to be slow. There had been so many tasks waiting to be done at once and most of them, of necessity, had to be done in stages. As he looked back he saw with pride how brilliant had been the Party strategy. Without delay they had concentrated on re-educating the People to new realistic ideas, lavishing the limited resources on the youth of the country in order to build the backbone of the revolution. And all the time there had been the constant Legislation to restrict the profits of the Foreign Capitalists.

Setbacks there had been, of course. He would not deny that. The Legislation for Higher Wages had not worried the big foreign investors after all. What had in fact happened had been that the cost of living had risen fantastically and it had been the poor man's businesses which had had to close down with the result that the trade had passed over to the big traders. This was not what the Party had intended at all. That had been a blunder which had only been overcome by restricting imports so that the Government became the sole agents for certain things. That had in the end been the master stroke.

But all the time there had been the baffling octopus of foreign investors. This land, that enterprise, this industry — all financed from overseas. What could be done? The Government had no money to buy them over.

So had come the Austerity and Freezing Plan, the belt tightening and then the big squeeze, the One Year Plan and the Overthrow.

A rationing scheme was introduced which forbade the purchase of all luxuries and allowed a very restricted buying of the essentials. This, coupled with a compulsory National Saving Scheme deducted at wage source, a freezing of assets and a suspension of most social service developments, created a considerable sum for the Treasury. Then the Party was ready for the Big Squeeze.

Unemployment had inevitably increased during that Austerity year. The People were angry. The Government was under criticism for its unfulfilled promises. Many had called for a fresh election or for the intervention of the Imperialist Power. It had been a near thing. Even the faith of the Party in its leaders had been sorely tried. It had been a precarious year, a nerve-racking year.

But at last everything was ready. The Party Agents had done their work well and they had managed to pull through to complete their plan. El Dragon had called them to face a year of Austerity. They had faced it. Now at last it was at an end. The First of August had come! "Let all who are employed by Foreign Enterprises come out on strike. The Party will look after your interests." In field and factory and mine all work ceased. The Government upheld the action of the strikers and at once brought into force an Unemployment Benefit Scheme authorising the use of the Funds accumulated during the year of Austerity. The anger of the People was appeased. They awaited the outcome of their challenge.

They did not demand higher wages or shorter hours or special privileges. They declared that they would not resume work until they could be shareholders in the industries in which they worked.

The effect was far more devastating than even the Party had estimated. The Foreigners decided with one accord to close down and leave. This is where El Dragon had lost some of his friends. They warned him that he was going too far and that the sudden loss of foreign capital would spell disaster.

"Let them go" he had said. "When they have gone we can take over and work the mines and reap the harvests of our own soil. The wealth of the land shall be the wealth of the People. This is what we have worked for through the years. This is our hour. There can be no going back now. The People shall come into their own."

The weeks went by and the People waited. Slowly they began to realise something of the significance of what was happening. The Foreigners were leaving, but they were dismantling their equipment and taking it with them.

The men gathered in the bars to talk about it.

"What did you expect?" asked some of the non-Party men. "If they brought the equipment in you can't prevent them taking it out if you don't pay for it. It's theirs."

The Party men thought differently. "They bought their equipment with money sweated out of the People. It rightly belongs to the People. Government must put a stop to equipment being taken out of the country while there is still some left or we will have no equipment to work with. It's an offence against the rights of the People to take away their means of livelihood."

"A bit late to talk about taking away the People's means of livelihood when the People have refused to work," said the non-Party men. "We are going to have nothing to work with and no work. What will happen when the Fund runs out? We'll be worse off than we were before.

Something obviously had to be done quickly, for not only were the Foreigners leaving but so were many of the wealthier lifelong inhabitants. El Dragon saw the spectre of National Bankruptcy hovering uncomfortably near, as some of his friends had warned. He had hoped at first that the Dock strike would have prevented the equipment from leaving the country, but the companies had brought in their own dismantlers.

It was at this stage that things had got out of hand. Some angered strikers had a brush with some of the foreign dismantlers and got injured. Like wildfire, exaggerated reports had circulated and the anger and frustration of the years burst out into violence. There were terrible things that are best forgotten. El Dragon wished that he himself could forget the horror of it. His wife had been about to step into a boat to return to town after a visit to a Party meeting and had been mistaken for a foreign fugitive trying to escape to one of the company steamers." A drunken striker swung his cutlass at her and before anyone could restrain him had literally cut her to pieces.

As long as he lived he would never forget the shock of seeing the mutilated remains, and to learn that the crime had been committed by one of his own people.

That had been months ago. They had been full and eventful months. The Imperialist Power had shown her authority. Warships had come and the situation had been very tense.

There had been consultations and much anxiety. El Dragon knew that the Imperialist Power had the authority to overrule his Government; indeed, threatened to do so. Some people said it would be a good thing.

El Dragon and other Ministers pointed out that all the recent changes had come through legislation. The decision to leave had been made by the foreigners themselves. The strikes, they maintained, had been the inevitable outcome of long-standing grievances. The People were not to be blamed. And now that the foreign investors had left there could no longer be justification for any sort of administration from overseas. There were no longer overseas interests to be looked after!

The Imperialists talked of millions of dollars poured into the development of the country and of further millions of dollars worth of property built by foreign funds.

"Let us govern ourselves," declared El Dragon. "Let us work to create our own industries. Let us stand on our own feet. Let us feel that the land belongs to us. Give us our independence."

To his amazement the Imperialists had given consent — conditionally. It was in effect to be a 'trial period independence' during which time the People must prove themselves, and during which time also the Imperialists Power could intervene in exceptional circumstances. There was also the further provision that no concession denied to the Imperialist Power should be granted to any other country.

El Dragon and his Government did hot hesitate. It was not altogether what they wanted but it was a start. They saw the possibilities.

Chapter 2.

So the great Day of Independence had come at last.

The day had been given over to rejoicing. The processions had been wonderful. The flag of the Republic had been unfurled. It had been a most moving ceremony. Then he had broadcast to the People. But the greatest moment of all had been when he had appeared on the balcony in all the dazzle of the floodlights. The memory of the mighty cheers rang in his ears over and over again. It had been an unforgettable day.

The clock struck three. Outside the revelry still continued. He turned to the window. There was a glow in the sky. He hoped the People would not go too far in their rejoicing. He hoped the Fire Brigades were sober and able to cope with the fire.

A few more hours and he must be at work again. There were tremendous tasks ahead.—

At last he drifted into sleep.

At 6 o'clock he was awakened. He would have gone to sleep again but a realisation of all that was at stake crowded into his drowsy thoughts. There were tasks that must be tackled without delay. The People were waiting for action. Yesterday in his radio message he had told them that the land was theirs. He had issued a stirring call to every man, woman and child to work together for the prosperity of all. But El Dragon realised only too well that he could no longer blame anybody else for the problems of the People. Oratory would be of little value in the days ahead. The People awaited 'The Plan'.

He ate a hurried meal and then for two hours with his secretary he dealt with urgent business. It amazed him what a vast amount of urgent business always seemed to accumulate. There was far too much to deal with for the time being. Much of it he had to declare 'not urgent' and 'to be dealt with later' and an irritating twinge of conscience reminded him that he was now beginning to do what he had always so vehemently condemned in the old regime — pigeon-holing.

Alarming reports were coming in all the time of damage done to property by the excesses of the celebrations of the previous day. He sent an urgent message to the Radio Station asking the People to restrain themselves, pointing out that all damage to property would cost the taxpayer money. At the thought of the Radio Station another uneasy thought crossed his mind. It was going to be an expensive luxury now that there were practically no capitalistic businesses to pay for the sponsored programmes. Where was the money to come from? — But he must not spend time on that problem, he decided. The Minister of Education must devise some competitive People's Programme scheme on some sort of lottery system so that the costs to the Government would be minimised. All the same, it was going to cost the Government a lot of money.

At 9am he called his Cabinet Meeting to analyse the situation and draw up a statement of policy. It was a terrible revelation.

With the withdrawal of foreign investors two-thirds of the population were unemployed. Hardly any of the remainder had productive employment. Many were redundant. It was a shock to everybody to learn that the Unemployment Benefit Fund would be exhausted in less than a month.

Food, they agreed, must be the first consideration. The People must be set to work on the land at once.

"What about wages?" asked one member of the Council. "The People came out on strike saying that they would not return unless they could share the profits. The wages have been going up and up. We have not got the resources to pay the scale of wages we demanded of the employers who have left."

"That is not as difficult as it sounds," replied El Dragon. "We will promise them shares in the profits. That is no problem. The truth is that there will be no profits for years to come, seeing that there is so much equipment to buy. Therefore we can confidently promise them shares. Promises will cost us nothing. As for wages, later on we can count on the Great Ally From Across the Seas to come to our assistance. We have a little capital in the Treasury.

We must make that go as far as possible. We can, for the time being, pay wages partly in "*Purchase Tickets*" which can be spent at Government-owned stores which we will set up. The profits at the Government stores will help to swell the Treasury.

"Will the stores be able to replenish their stocks with *Purchase Tickets*?" asked a member.

"Let us not look for imaginary obstacles," El Dragon replied. "Remember we are only making emergency plans. The stocks at present in the stores will last a little while."

"How long?"

"We will have that investigated, Comrade. Now let us move on —"

"Just a moment" interjected another. "We have made plans for the unemployed agriculturalists, but what of the thousands of mechanics and office workers and people like them who are drawing unemployment benefit now that the foreign businesses have closed down?"

"They will have to take whatever work is offered to them. Party members who have office experience we will try to absorb into departmental work. In time, businesses will develop again and there will be scope for the others. For the time being it will do them no harm to have a little manual labour."

"Hear, hear," agreed several. Others were silent.

Then came the vexed question of communications and overseas trade. The Council settled down to examine the extent of the Government's resources. There was no Air Force. The fleet consisted of ten boats, mostly old, and a few motorboats. The land resources consisted of an obsolete railway, a few lorries, and a few dozen cars reserved for Ministers and Government Officials.

"Well, Comrades," declared El Dragon. "That is the position. We have to face it squarely. The People, too, must be shown the gravity of the situation and realise that they must make sacrifices. There can be no more pleasure trips. Our ships must be used for commerce only. The small boats must do the passenger ferrying. It is clear that to keep such traffic to a minimum 'passes' will have to be obtained for such journeys."

"That will create a bit of employment, anyhow," remarked one member, "issuing and checking passes."

El Dragon was not amused. "The position will not remain as serious as this for long. The People must build their own ships. This will be our new great industry." (Prolonged cheers)

"We will set our unemployed cutting timber and building houses and building ships." (more cheers).

"And I suppose part of the wages will be paid for in *'Purchase Tickets'* as for the agriculturalists?"

"Precisely".

So, the day wore on until preliminary plans were sufficiently shaped out to make a public pronouncement.

To say that the People were shocked was to put it mildly. They had not formerly considered how deficient their country was in equipment and finance. Many decided at once to leave the country and set off for the shipping offices. They had forgotten of course, that ships had ceased to call now that the former business had ceased to export. There were no ships. The country had achieved Independence. It was debated hotly in the bars that night.

Another topic arose from this realisation of independence. If ships were not calling to take commerce away, they would bring none in!

Overnight the stores ran out of stocks of imported goods. A new industry began — a Black Market in scarce commodities.

Chapter 3.

El Dragon was worried. The Plan was not working as smoothly as had been hoped. People were not very pleased with the idea of *Purchase Tickets*. It had become necessary to double the Police Force to keep down the looting which had broken out.

The People on the land were already complaining about the lack of equipment. The distasteful decision had to be made: some of the meagre resources would have to be used to obtain the equipment so urgently required. Republic currency was an urgent necessity, for coins were fast disappearing from circulation. But the Republic possessed inadequate equipment for the making of currency. This great wall seemed to appear before them wherever they looked — inadequate tools and inadequate resources to obtain them.

Not only that; the radio programmes were not going too well. People were demanding payment for their services. Now and then people got on the air who said sarcastic and uncomplimentary things, and so a censorship had become necessary — and that, of course, meant higher costs. The cost of administration and surveying had reached alarming proportions. There would have to be cuts!

The roads, fortunately, did not require much attention, for there was scarcely any traffic these days. Not much to be saved there. The big cut would have to be in education. The teachers would have to show their patriotism by accepting salary reductions. They must make sacrifices like the rest of the community. Further, the Government could only afford to pay the teachers in the Government School. For the future, schools owned by religious bodies must shoulder the entire expense. Now that films no longer came into the country the cinemas could be used as community centres and for Party demonstrations.

The Churches at once said that they could not pay the teachers and would have to close down. This simplified things a great deal, for the Government could now blame the Churches for causing unemployment. But to his surprise El Dragon found that the People were not as angry as he had expected. They realised that the Churches had spoken the truth. They could not pay the teachers unless money came from foreign countries. The children organised their own schools — and did they have fun! Further increases in the Police Force became necessary and it began to appear that the cost of having no school was likely to be greater than the cost of maintaining the normal educational system.

The shipbuilding programme was a little slow in starting and the wage bill was alarming.

The Minister of Transport announced that there was sufficient gasoline for one week only. It became obvious that all new ships would have to be sailing or wood-burning vessels. It was all very humiliating, but finally the decision had to be made: 'Only Ministers shall be permitted the use of private cars. All road haulage must be by animal drawn vehicles.'

The price of donkeys rose rapidly. All-night guards had to be employed to protect the precious beasts.

The Minister of Health came to him one day with pages of statistics. El Dragon was very tired. He did not want to see them. "But you must," pleaded the Minister. "The death rate is rising rapidly. Our medical supplies are almost exhausted. Epidemics are becoming more and more frequent. Something must be done before things get any worse."

"What are the minimum precautions that can be taken to prevent further decline?" asked El Dragon.

"Well, Chief," went on the Minister, "You haven't heard the whole story yet. You see, since the Drug Stores have had no patent medicines the conditions at our dispensaries have become chronic. We will have to set up hundreds of clinics, guarantee supplies of medicines each week and essential equipment—"

El Dragon began to get impatient, "And is there anything else?"

"Yes, Chief, we must close the drink trade."

"What?" replied El Dragon. "It can't be done. The People wouldn't stand for it. It is the one thing that keeps them quiet and anyhow it is about our only source of revenue."

"It must be done," persisted the Minister. "With the continued rise in the cost of living, the People are eating an inadequate diet and excess of alcohol is playing havoc with people's constitutions. At the very least, Chief, you must limit the sale of drink. Why not ration it in some way? Say, have a special kind of *Purchase Ticket* for the stuff which could only be obtained by doing a certain amount of extra work?"

"It can't be done, I'm afraid," said El Dragon dismally.

"Why not?" asked the Minister.

"Because I have just learned from the Treasury that the *Purchase Tickets* returned by the Stores exceed the number which have so far been officially printed. Someone is making a fortune out of printing *Purchase Tickets*."

Chapter 4.

El Dragon rode his horse down the Main Street of the Capital flanked by four Police Officers. The People had shown their disapproval of Ministers riding in cars since 'The Fund' had run out and in any case, there was a certain dignity in the Leader of the Republic riding a horse.

It was the silence of the People that hurt him, though. At the beginning they had cheered him wherever he went. Now they either looked at him sadly or muttered angrily. He must have the Party publicity methods overhauled. People were openly blaming the Government. Some other source of blame must be found to divert criticism. There would have to be a few people found guilty of sabotage.

The money-raising schemes had been a sheer waste of time. The State Lottery had yielded twenty-one dollars and nine hundred and seven *Purchase Tickets*. Revenue from taxation was negligible. All Customs profits had ceased long before. El Dragon yearned for the appearance of a money-raising genius.

The old steamers were doing their best to carry on trade with their neighbouring countries but the exports did little more than procure the weekly medical supplies. The Minister of Health had been quite right in his prophecy. But it had not been necessary to stop the Drink Trade. People ceased to visit the Bars. They made their own!

If only the machinery would come. There had been so many irritating hold-ups. The makers had asked questions about security. Somehow the whole world seemed to know that former 'foreign owners' of businesses within the Republic had not been paid for their property when they had been 'bought over'. The Republic did not carry a good name.

If only the mines could be put on a satisfactory footing. But something seemed to be wrong there, too. He would have to see that only Party men were employed there. He must avoid risks.

El Dragon had not confided in the others how disappointed he was that the Great Ally Across the Seas had done nothing yet. At the outset he had sent Representatives and when at last they had returned they had been most optimistic. Yes, they assured him, the Great Ally would help their young comrades to get on their feet.

But the help had not materialised. It was apparently a question of priorities. The Great Ally was already helping so many. There were so many great projects already in hand. But the message had come, 'Be of good courage, we will not let you sink.'

The dark city streets at night were getting quite a problem since electricity had been cut down. The food and clothing stores, particularly, needed extra guards and there were far too many non-party meetings. Workers were becoming insolent to their overseers and there was strike talk. The children were getting out of hand. It had been most embarrassing when they had broken into Police Headquarters and tied up every officer, marking each with a sign of a skull-and-crossbones.

He was disturbed, too, to receive reports of frontier incidents with bold Vascalians who had taken certain liberties within the borders of the Republic. One of these had been arrested and brought to the Capital for interrogation. He was quite defiant, saying that he was a tourist and as no facilities existed within the Republic for the help of tourists, he had been obliged to make his own way across the country. His arrest while admiring the beautiful scenery was known to certain friends who had been with him at the time of arrest. They would without doubt inform his government of his harsh treatment.

El Dragon acted very wisely. He had the man released and escorted back in the most comfortable launches and donkey carts available.

It was a good thing that in recent months El Dragon had had the foresight to arrange for unemployed Party members to have military training. As a result, the Republican army numbered over 3,700.

It would have been much larger if it had not been restricted to Party members. It was, however, unfortunate that they could not be provided with proper uniforms; but the clothing situation was now becoming serious.

Unfortunately, too, their equipment in terms of arms was equally scarce. Ammunition was so low that it could not be used for training purposes. The Republican Navy consisted of Police Boats armed with rifles. All very alarming; but then, what could be done in the circumstances?

It was at about the same time that he discovered that large-scale smuggling was going on. Gold and diamonds were going out of the Republic faster than they were reaching the Treasury.

El Dragon had no alternative. The country had to be put under Martial Law.

Chapter 5.

The first People's boats were at last launched. In the end it had been decided that they would have to be sailing barges with provision for twelve long oars. The crews consisted of Party men who acted as navigators and labour overseers, together with oarsmen drawn from the overfull prisons. These boats were designed chiefly for transporting timber down the rivers. El Dragon had plans for larger ships, with thirty-six oars in two tiers such as he had admired in one of the few remaining schoolbooks, but his friends had advised against it. "People will start talking of slavery if you do that," they had pointed out.

The streets of the city were a queer sight these days. The horse-drawn saloon cars had been popular at first until the supply of tyres had become exhausted. Now, passengers who could afford the luxury travelled in coolie handcarts since all animal-drawn vehicles were required for transporting materials.

Negotiations for machinery had finally broken down. There was found to be insufficient money to pay for it. In desperation, the Grand Council had decided that somehow they must spare enough money to send another envoy to the Great Ally Across the Sea to beg for immediate help. It was a moving thing to see how the comrades of the Party brought forth the best of their wardrobes in order to ensure that their envoy was adequately dressed for his mission.

Meanwhile the agricultural schemes were making some progress, especially since Party men equipped with revolvers and whips had been appointed overseers. The hours of labour had had to be increased, of course, but, as was pointed out to the labourers, the Republic was at a point of crisis. They were all fighting for survival.

"Survival of what?" someone had asked. Unfortunately, he had asked it in a somewhat aggressive manner and so lost his status in the community and his share of *Purchase Tickets*. He became an oarsman on the next new boat.

Frontier incidents were on the increase. The number of tourists who strayed into the Republic became quite considerable. Members of the Council were of the opinion that it might have some relation to the smuggling of gold and diamonds, but as they were all Party men who were in charge of the mines it seemed scarcely conceivable. Investigations were made, but no evidence was forthcoming.

People were beginning to comment on the fact that Party men were seemingly able to find means of purchasing the best houses, and even obscure Party men had meat in their diet. El Dragon had quickly squashed the latter rumour in one of his broadcasts. Why, there was scarcely any meat in the country these days. Then he had gone on to talk of the great achievements of the Fishing Fleet; how the quantity of fish caught had increased tremendously since Party men had supervised. The Minister of Health had followed with an enlightening talk on the high food value of fish for which he was greatly complimented by his Chief.

"That was a fine pep talk, Comrade, it will boost up morale no end," he said as they walked out of the studio and made their way to the waiting coolie carts. (El Dragon only used his horse now on public occasions as it was needed for road haulage).

The Minister of Health made no reply. He hardly knew how to explain to his Chief that only Party men ate the fish. There was no ice anyhow to keep it fresh and salt was unobtainable. For a long time he had wanted to tell his Chief of the desperate medical situation. The Party-trained Doctors were just no good. They diagnosed every case as fever or blood pressure and would prescribe no medicine except at fantastic prices. People were ceasing to go to the Doctors and there were no Drug Stores. To his amazement, the People were healthier than he had ever known them. But he kept his thoughts to himself. The situation was fluid. Ministers were becoming redundant lately. Only the previous week the Minister of Education had gone out of Office now that education was confined to those Church Schools which provided a voluntary system of unpaid teachers. The ex-Minister now supervised the training of the Police Intelligence Department.

It had been a good thing that the Police had been able to trace the printers of the counterfeit *Purchase Tickets*. It had baffled the Council for a long time. Even when they had confiscated every Printing Press the racket still went on. In the end it was discovered that there was a perpetual mistake in the book-keeping and the Chief of the Party Printing Department became an oarsman.

The frontier incidents became more serious. There were some unfortunate clashes and complaints were received from the Government of Vascalia. It was shortly after this that El Dragon had to explain in one of his now infrequent broadcasts that it had been discovered that there was a serious error in the maps showing the boundaries between the Republic and Vascalia. Actually, he explained, a considerable portion of what had always been thought of as Republican territory was in fact Vascalian territory. It was of course, one of the many errors of the old regime, which, as the People knew well, had been thoroughly untrustworthy. Government, he went on, was also considering leasing other portions of territory to the neighbouring state of Bombador in exchange for certain trading concessions. Those citizens of the Republic living in the areas involved could choose to move back into the parts of the Republic remaining or could stay where they were under the administration of Bombador. He pointed out that there would be language difficulties.

There were language difficulties; which resulted in the problem of having too many oarsmen for the too few boats. It was remarkable, also, to realise how much they had underestimated the population of the ceded territories.

Everybody was getting anxious about the progress of their envoy to the Great Ally Across the Seas. Months had gone by and there had been no word. The closer proximity of Vascalia and Bombador made assistance a matter of extreme urgency. In view of the shortage of ammunition, the Minister of Sea Wall and Land Defences advocated archery as part of the army training.

With the rare importation of paper, reading matter became more and more scarce. It was a source of great surprise therefore to see how many citizens were reading in these days and reading with great attention. El Dragon, coming early to a Council meeting one day, found a Group of Ministers poring over a document spread on the table before them.

"Hello, what have you got there?" he asked, "Another set of statistics?"

"Not exactly, Chief" replied one. "It is something that came in a parcel from the last steamer that brought medical supplies. It had no address on it and the crew walked off with most of it. On enquiry I learned that quite a few packages come each trip and the men take them to their homes and pass them around."

"But this is dangerous," exclaimed El Dragon. "Can't you see what this is? This is propaganda to overthrow the Republic. This is seditious literature. It must be banned."

Chapter 6.

El Dragon had just been conducted around the armament factory where the blacksmiths were fashioning mighty swords and formidable-looking pikes. Yes, there was no doubt about it, the Minister of the Sea Wall and Land Defences was doing a fine job with his limited resources. He was certainly a man with ideas: a progressive.

El Dragon had been greatly touched when he had been taken on one side, "A special present; for your birthday, Chief," said the Minister. El Dragon gazed in delight on the beautiful suit of shining armour that had been specially made for him. He had tried it on there and then and everyone had looked on with admiration. At once all the other Ministers placed a personal order.

This was progress. Another new industry had been born.

Then El Dragon had watched the archers. They really were a fine body of men and he had to admit that he was proud of them. The Minister had also wanted to show him his new corps of blow-pipe men but El Dragon reminded him that they were already late for the Council meeting and they had nearly a mile to walk to get to it.

It was a very important Council meeting. There still had been no word from the envoy to the Great Ally Across the Seas and even the Party men were getting restive and critical.

"It is not right," said one Minister when this subject on the agenda was discussed. "I let him have my best suit and he has not sent one word since he left."

"Yes, I am getting very anxious, too," said the Minister of Health, "He has got my only pair of underpants."

"Now, now, comrades," said El Dragon. "Those losses are, of course, greatly to be regretted but the chief problem is a very serious one for the Republic. We have waited in vain for help from the Great Ally Across the Sea. What is operating in my mind is this. It is probable that our envoy did not reach his destination."

A great hush fell upon the room as he went on. "Comrades, what I believe has happened is that somehow the Imperialist Power got wind of his mission and kidnapped him. It is the sort of thing we can expect of them." The men groaned at the thought of the loss of their precious clothing. "There is only one solution," went on El Dragon. "I must go myself, and I must go in disguise."

There was a dismayed silence in the council. The members looked at each other and swallowed hard. They knew what was coming next.

"Well, comrades," persisted El Dragon. "I know I can rely on you. What about it?" and he began to outline the wardrobe he would need. "You must scour the community if necessary." He turned to the Minister of Supply. "What have you got in the Depository?" (The Depository was the collecting centre for goods confiscated from the oarsmen before they were appointed to their respective boats).

The Minister of Supply shuffled his feet. "I am afraid Chief you won't find much there."

"Oh," asked El Dragon with some severity, "and why not?"

"We forgot to tell you," explained the Minister of Supply, "that the women made a raid on the Depository last week and took all the clothing. The men were powerless."

"The men were powerless?" shouted El Dragon incredulously, "Where was the Army and the Police?"

"Well, Chief," explained the minister. "They were the wives of the military and they said they were going to start a rebellion if they didn't get some clothes. We didn't tell you, Chief, because we knew you were worried."

The Party really did respond nobly to their leader's appeal and the day arrived for the departure of El Dragon in one of the timber ships which carried on a trade with the island of Threepops. It was an impressive departure. The guard of honour formed an archway of pikes as he walked down the gangplank. Many citizens, as well as Party men, turned out to see him go. He did not hear a discordant word from any of them. The citizens were held back at a distance of about fifty yards and the Party men cheered him all the time until the boat was in midstream.

To be honest, there had, as a matter of fact, been a certain amount of criticism from the People who said that so much money had already been spent on the visit of the envoy some months before that it was unwise to spend money now when it could be put to better use within the Republic. No, they were not trying to show disloyalty, but it was a matter of economics. But the Council had agreed that the journey should be undertaken and who better to intercede with the Great Ally From Across the Seas than El Dragon?

So El Dragon set out from the Republic on his momentous mission.

Chapter 7.

His first port of call was Threepops and he at once began to make enquiries about his envoy. People seemed a little puzzled at first, then someone threw light on the whole mystery. "Why, yes. I remember now. That was the man who called a Press conference as soon as he arrived and then the next day sold his First Class ticket and opened a little business selling gold and diamonds and that sort of thing. He made a small fortune in a few weeks. He used to go down to meet "*The Ark*" every time it came in."

"*The Ark*?" queried El Dragon.

"Yes, that old boat you have just come in on."

"Oh," said El Dragon, somewhat abashed. "He used to meet the ship, did he?" and his mouth set in a hard line.

"Yes, but he got caught in the end. Smuggling and Customs evasion, and that sort of thing. He is still in prison."

El Dragon thanked the man for the information and decided that there were certain investigations that would have to be carried out when he returned to the Republic. He realised all the more what a pity it had been that the Republic had not been able to afford to continue telephonic communication with the outside world. He ought to have learned these facts months before. He had been fooled and that was one thing which he could not stand.

By devious routes he at last reached the Great Ally and after certain embarrassing misunderstandings had been cleared up he at last gained an audience with the great Blinkersov himself.

Blinkersov was very sympathetic and understanding and El Dragon admired the way in which he asked questions which showed that he had a real interest in the Republic. He asked questions about the mineral resources of the country, the strength of the armed forces, naval and air bases. He enquired also about the wealth of the neighbouring countries and the quality of the frontier guard."

El Dragon explained the difficulties he had experienced over boundaries.

"Yes, my young friend", the Great Blinkersov sympathised, "You have obviously been greatly imposed upon and, as you say, it would be a waste of time to put the matters before the United Nations. It is obvious, Comrade Dragon, that we must come personally to your help. Mind you," he went on, "it will be useless to toy with the situation. We will have to help in a big way." El Dragon breathed a sigh of relief. He had not failed his People. He was succeeding in his mission.

The Great Blinkersov went on, "First of all, we will send a team of experts who will survey the territory and report back. Then we will soon get things moving satisfactorily. Yes, we will soon get the matter in hand. It must be understood," he went on, "that when we come in we must have a free hand if we are really to help you."

"Quite, quite," agreed El Dragon readily. "There is of course our agreement with the Imperialist Power. There might be objections —"

"Bah! Don't let that worry you," assured Blinkersov. "Just leave that to us. We have a system that always works. What we will do in this case will be to liberate Vascalia and Bombador, building roads and equipping your Republic in the process. The Imperialist Power will protest and we will negotiate and argue for several years, at the end of which time they will agree to us becoming the Protector of either Vascalia or Bombador and then everyone will be better off."

"A brilliant scheme," breathed the awed El Dragon. "You have given me new hope. I shall go back to my People inspired."

"Good, good!" smiled Blinkersov, "Now let me see. Ah, let me look at my diary. Um—I must give you time to get back and there are certain other little projects that I must complete first. Well, shall we say April 1st. My party of experts will arrive in your country on April 1st."

"That will be fine," agreed El Dragon.

"That is all arranged then," went on Blinkersov. "Now tell me, is there anything else I can do for you?"

"Well," asked El Dragon, a little embarrassed. "We have certain shortages," and we have insufficient capital to import. Can you — I am wondering — have you any old cups and saucers you have finished with?" A little afraid that he had been too daring he hastened to add, "It doesn't matter if they are chipped, but, you see, things are so hard —"

"Certainly, certainly, Comrade," the Great Blinkersov assured him, "No trouble at all."

El Dragon left the land of the Great Ally in jubilation and chafed at the slowness of the journey home. He just could not seem to be able to travel fast enough. His stay in the land of the Great Ally had proved more expensive than he had ever believed possible and he found the crate of chinaware very tiresome as he tramped through one country after another. At least he had the great good fortune to get a stoker's job on a tramp steamer bound for Threepops and he felt that his trials were at an end. Now all would be well. Soon he would be home again. Soon his People would be welcoming him. He had succeeded!

Arrived in Threepops, he enquired at once for the Republican steamer.

"Sorry, chum," explained the Port Officer, "But we haven't seen '*The Ark*' for nearly three months now."

"What?" exclaimed El Dragon in amazement, "Has she been sunk?"

"Oh, no," replied the Officer, "The last I heard of her was that she and two other Republican ships were running a private service off the coast of Vascalia."

"Oh, indeed," commented El Dragon. He was glad that the Officer did not seem to recognise him. "Then what am I going to do? I must get back to the Republic without delay."

"You must be a fool," declared the officer, "Anybody who wants to get back to the Republic is a fool. Nobody goes back there."

El Dragon explained that he had certain personal reasons.

"Well," said the Officer, lowering his voice. "This is in strict confidence, but as a matter of fact we have a little boat which goes over there quite frequently. Gold and diamonds, you know. We might be able to arrange to take you across. You must understand that we will not be able to take you into port. You will have to land somewhere along the coast and make your way as best you can, but at any rate, you will be able to get into the Republic."

Chapter 8.

The voyage to the Republic proved to be quite exciting. The boat kept away from the coast until nightfall and then crept up to an island at the mouth of one of the great rivers.

"Why all the secrecy?" El Dragon asked one of the crew. "I didn't know there were any close patrols along the coast."

"Oh, no," came the reply. "It isn't the patrols that we have to keep our eyes open for. The Party men are all right. We don't have any trouble with them. It is the People who make things awkward."

"The People! Why the People?" enquired El Dragon.

"Man, don't you realise what we have got in these bales? This ship is full of clothing and flour. If the People saw us they would tear us to pieces to get them. No, we deal with Party men. We should get four thousand dollars worth of gold and diamonds for this lot, barring accidents. Now just keep quiet. We are going inshore."

It was quite an exciting experience for El Dragon as he assisted the crew in furtively carrying the sacks and bales ashore. Finally, the transaction was complete and the boat vanished into the night. At last he stood upon his native soil again.

He could not recognise any of the Party men and thought it inadvisable to reveal his identity. It would soon be daybreak, so, getting his directions from the smugglers he shouldered his box and set off along the track. It was not until he had been walking for half an hour that he realised that he was on an island. His problems, obviously, were still not ended.

It took him ten whole days to make his way to the capital and he was thankful for the beard which he had grown since he had left the land of the Great Ally.

He had lost his jacket on the first day and his shoes on the second when he had been foolish enough to travel through a village instead of around it. On both occasions he had been interrogated by village councils who decreed that it was not in the interests of the Republic for any man to be so well dressed when the rest of the community had to make do with lags and sacking. Fortunately he had been able to hide his box in the ditch on each occasion.

At last the Capital was in sight. Just one more river to cross and then all would be well.

But even within sight of his goal he discovered that it was not going to be so easy after all. The Party man operating the canoe would not be put off with promises. It cost El Dragon his shirt and hat before the boat got under way.

On the other side of the river they saw him coming and a deputation awaited him as he stepped ashore. With a great sense of elation he stepped forward smiling broadly. The officials ignored him. They were only interested in his box and pounced upon it at once.

"What have we here?" exclaimed the Chief Landing Officer excitedly and ripped off the boards. The other men opened their mouths in astonishment. "Cups and saucers!" they exclaimed incredulously.

"My, my. Just a minute," said the Chief Landing Officer fetching a tattered book. "Let me see — cups — yes, here it is — Yes, young fella, you will have to pay customs duty on these at the rate of one dollar for each piece. Comrades, we must send a message to the Treasury at once. This will about double the Country's resources. Come on, young fella, a dollar on each of them or they will be confiscated."

"But they are cracked," protested El Dragon.

"So are you," replied the Officer amid laughter.

El Dragon waited until the laughter had ceased then drew himself up proudly. "I am El Dragon," he declared.

At this the men simply shrieked with laughter. "El Dragon, they kept repeating and laughed till the tears ran down their cheeks.

"El Dragon!" said the Chief Officer when the laughter had subsided somewhat, "You are about the ninth to tell us that tale. Come on, you fellas, we'd better put him in the Depository till the Chief decides what to do with him."

So El Dragon found himself inside the Depository, without the cups and saucers which he had carried so carefully for thousands of miles.

The interior of the Depository occasioned him a great deal of surprise. It did not contain confiscated goods, as he had expected: but people. Lots of people. They greeted him with very little interest as he stood where his captors had thrust him, just inside the barred door. The light was not very good, so the inmates had not a good view of him. It was very hot and smelled unbearably. El Dragon turned to an old man reclining with his back to the wall and asked how long it was likely to be before he would get an interview with the Chief.

"Interview with the Chief?" he repeated in amazement and spat. "You're not likely to get one while you are in here. The best you are likely to get is a life sentence on the river galleys."

"Indeed," said El Dragon blankly. This was not the homecoming he had visualised. After all he had done for the country! He decided to learn as much as he could.

"What are you in here for?" he asked.

"Reporting a Party crook," replied the old man.

"I see," said El Dragon. "But I suppose you will be able to get things straightened out in the People's Courts?"

"In what?" shouted the man.

"In court," repeated El Dragon. "Are there no non-Party magistrates?"

The old man turned away in disgust. "It's no good talking to a fool like you. You're living in a different age. You had better go to sleep again."

El Dragon was silent for a while. He recalled that, a long time before, the Magistrates had been replaced by Party men. He began to reconnoitre to see if there was any chance of escaping. If only he could get a message out. At last he mustered courage to ask someone for a piece of paper. The men within earshot howled with laughter. "You'll have to manage without paper," they told him.

"But I want to write a message," he persisted.

The men looked at him incredulously. "Who is this fella? He must be daft," said one and thereafter they ignored him.

El Dragon was determined that he would get out of that building somehow. A close examination of the walls showed that there were some rotting boards high up on the eastern side. If several people climbed on each other's shoulders, he thought, it should be possible to work on the weak spot until a hole was made large enough for a human body to pass through. He decided that something must be done without delay. He must find a way to organise the prisoners but first of all he would have to gain their confidence. He would have to act with great tact and caution. He paced the floor for some time in silence.

Suddenly he stopped in the centre of the floor and clapped his hands then strode to one end of the shed, "Comrades," he addressed them, "Are you satisfied?"

The response was totally unexpected. It was as if he had put a match to a barrel of gunpowder. Everybody began to talk at once, abusing the Republic, abusing the Party, abusing the Leaders.

"Just a minute, men—" he inflected, but nobody heard him. They were all fully occupied in giving vent to their feelings. It was quite clear to him now that it was a good thing that they did not recognise him as El Dragon. To stop the flow of abuse seemed impossible and he stood there bewildered.

It was stopped very effectively, however, by some hard blows on the door. The Party Guards outside made a few choice threats and all was quiet.

"There you are," pointed out El Dragon quietly, "That shows you that is not the right way to go about things. We must plan carefully."

The men nodded agreement. This man had sense.

Seizing his opportunity, El Dragon began again. "Comrades, let me introduce myself. My name doesn't matter, but if you like you can call me Fitz. Now listen. You have noticed already how much I am out of touch with things. Well, the truth is that I have been out of the country for some time. A few days ago I came back—"

"I said the fella was a fool," interjected the old man. "If a fella gets out of the Republic, he must have something wrong with him to come back."

"Ah!" went on El Dragon, quick to retrieve his mistake, "I have come back to help you."

"What?" said one incredulously, "To help us get rid of the Party?"

El Dragon swallowed hard. He had not been quite prepared for this one. He began again. "Comrades, I have come to bring you hope. Help is coming. In a week or so there will be a great change in your prospects. But the time is short. We must prepare without delay."

He had noticed the rising enthusiasm of the men and at this remark they crowded round him to shake his hand. "Fitz is the man for us," they cried. "At last we have got a leader who will set us free from the exploitation of the Party."

"Fitz," declared a young man known as Chip. "For months we have been waiting for leadership. The country is waiting. It will rise at your call."

El Dragon could see that he would have to move very carefully, and changed the subject quickly.

"We must lay our plans carefully," he went on. "We must wait until it is dark then climb up and break through those rotten boards."

"Why wait until it is dark?" asked Chips, "There's no harm in starting to work them loose now."

"That's right," agreed another, and without delay the younger men set to work and the older men began to make detailed plans for the future. El Dragon felt it best not to contribute too many ideas. He must allow events to take their course.

Darkness came at last. The escape proved an easy matter. A small party of young men climbed through the opening and in a few minutes had unbarred the door.

"What of the guards?" asked El Dragon.

"Don't worry about them," assured the men. "They are in the river."

"Can they swim?"

"We didn't stop to ask them. No, I don't think they'll be able to," and they laughed. "But, come on, don't let's stay here. We must keep moving."

El Dragon was waiting for an opportunity to slip away, but his plans were frustrated by the zeal of the men. "There is no moon for a while yet and it's dark," said Chip. "Mind how you go, Fitz," and a man walked on either side of him to guide and support him.

In a short while they reached their destination, a disused Fire Station in the centre of the town. "We'll be alright here," said the old man showing him to a room which had once been an office. "You get some sleep, Fitz. We'll keep a guard to see that you are not disturbed. Meanwhile we'll pass the word around. Let's see, what date did you say your friends would be arriving?"

"April 1st," replied El Dragon quietly.

"April 1st. Right. That's fine. But, let's see, what is the date today?"

Nobody knew and the old man explained that no almanacs had been issued since paper ran out. The date was put on a notice board at the Town Hall for any who might be interested. "We will send someone along in the morning to find out," he added.

El Dragon thanked him and retired to his room. He noticed that the windows were securely boarded up. He was in a tough spot. He had better wait a bit.

He listened to the sound of departing footsteps at short intervals until after a while all was quiet. He waited a bit longer then crept to the door and softly opened it. At once somebody jumped up. "Is there anything you want, Chief?" asked the man eagerly. El Dragon saw that it was Chip.

"How many are there here?" asked El Dragon.

"Six of us," was the reply.

"I see," said El Dragon and thought for a few moments before he went on. "Now tell me. Since you say there is no writing paper in the Republic, what does a man do if he wants to send a message?"

"Well," replied Chip, "He just says it and someone repeats it."

El Dragon realised it was not going to be easy. "Yes, of course, but supposing it was a long message."

"The messenger would have to remember it, Chief."

"But he might get the message wrong."

"Yes, that's right, Chief, he might."

"Well," persisted El Dragon, "Say somebody wanted to send a message a long, long way and the messenger wasn't able to go that far?"

"Then he would have to find another messenger to pass it on."

El Dragon was getting desperate. "But listen, Comrade, suppose someone wanted to write down a message he didn't want the messenger to know, what would he do then?"

"He'd get a different messenger."

This was getting hopeless. El Dragon tried once more. "Suppose he had no choice of messenger. He had to use whoever he could get to send it?"

"Oh, I get you," said Chip brightly. "You mean the Party Postal System. But that is only for Party men — officially."

"But what is that?"

"Well, what they do is they get a piece of smooth clay and write a message with a pointed stick and bake it hard to preserve it. Then, if it is very private they put it in a special box."

"Do you know where I can get one of those boxes?" asked El Dragon eagerly.

"No, only the Party men have them. I can get you some clay, though, if you want to do some writing," Chip offered.

Suddenly El Dragon had a brainwave. "Can you read?" he asked.

"Me?" Chip asked. "No, what's the use? There's nothing to read."

"Well, get me some clay, then, as soon as you can, will you, Comrade?"

"Right, Chief, but you'll have to wait till morning.

Chapter 9.

El Dragon was awakened the next morning by his loyal bodyguard Chip, bringing him a handful of food. "Here you are, Boss. I'm going to send one of the other men for the clay."

"Oh, don't do that," said El Dragon hurriedly. "The fewer people who know about it the better."

Chip looked puzzled. "But Chief, they are all your friends."

"Ah, yes" went on El Dragon, "But you see, this is all part of the plan and it is so delicate that there must be absolute secrecy. Look, Chip. This is my plan. I am going to pretend to be El Dragon and I am going to pretend to the Party that on April 1st, when my friends come, they are representatives of the Great Ally, see?"

"Gee, that's a clever plan, Chief."

"Now, listen," went on El Dragon. "You can see now why I want to write a message. I will write to the acting Leader of the Republic telling him that representatives of the Great Ally are coming and that they must make plans to welcome them. I will also tell them that I am a prisoner and I'll name a place on the other side of the country so that a lot of the troops going to rescue me will be out of town when our friends arrive. That will make it easier, won't it?"

Chip grinned in admiration, "Why, you are a genius, Chief."

"Right," said El Dragon, "Go get the clay as quick as you can."

Chip hurried off and El Dragon noticed to his disappointment that a group of his bodyguards had his room well under control. He would have to wait.

It was well over an hour before Chip returned with a lump of soft clay. The rest of the men eyed him curiously when he returned with the strange object. "What do you want that for Chief?" someone called out.

This was going to be awkward. "Well," said El Dragon. "I like to eat my food off a plate so I thought, while I have nothing to do I would make a plate out of clay and bake it."

Some of the men snorted in disgust, "Coconuts and bananas don't need plates."

"Ah, but if we get some rice," pointed out another, "When we have got rid of the Party men, then it would be a good idea to have some plates. Fitz has got some foresight. He is looking forward to the day when the People will be allowed to be civilized again."

They left him alone for a while after that and he was able to make a start in smoothing the surface in readiness for his message.

He was just about to begin when some of the leaders appeared. "Come for a conference," explained the old man. "Things are working nicely, Fitz," he went on. "First of all we have found out that today is March 23rd. We have just sent off messengers to every part of the Republic which it is possible to reach in a week, with instructions to tell the People to be ready for April 1st. The People will find ways of seeing that as many Party men as possible will be kept out of town when your friends come."

"Good work," said El Dragon, but inwardly his heart sank. The situation was getting worse and worse.

"We are also arranging," went on the old man, "For messengers to go to all people within two days journey and organise them into companies to march on the capital. They will mingle with the city crowd. When your friends arrive, then as soon as you give the signal they will attack."

"And what will the signal be?" asked El Dragon.

"The signal will be when you shake hands with the leader of the visitors."

"But how will that be possible?"

"Don't you worry about that. We'll fix it," the old man assured him.

It was a very bewildered El Dragon who, after the planning committee had gone an hour later, sat down to write his secret message.

Very laboriously El Dragon worked away at the clay. It was not as easy as he had anticipated. His letters proved to be too large so that he had to make the message short and that is where a big problem arose. He needed to convey so many points in the message. Somehow he had to convey the need for preparing the best possible hospitality for the visitors from the Great Ally; he wanted them to know of his own predicament, and the danger in which the Party stood, and altogether the urgency of the situation. It was quite plain that it was no easy task.

After several attempts he wrote the following: — *ALLY FROM ACROSS THE SEA ARRIVES APRIL 1st. ARRANGE HOSPITALITY. PLOT AGAINST PARTY. IMPRISONED. FIRE STATION. EL DRAGON.*

His bodyguards kept coming in to see how he was getting on with his plate making and he had to explain that he was just experimenting with the clay to start with. There was no real hurry for the plates. The men did not seem very impressed.

At last, at about midday he was finished. He called Chip in and showed him the outcome of his labours.

"Can you read what this says?" he asked, trying to conceal the note of anxiety from his voice.

"No, Boss," replied Chip, "It just looks like a lot of marks to me. Do you want me to put it in the sun now to bake it?"

"No, no," replied El Dragon hastily, "The wrong people might read it. No, you must take it just as it is. But you must be very careful how you handle it for if it gets crushed it will be ruined. Keep it hidden. Don't let anyone see it is a message until you get to the office of the Leader of the Republic. Then just hand it over."

"O.K. Boss, you just leave it to me. I'll wrap it in a banana leaf, will that do?"

"Excellent," said El Dragon, patting him on the back. "This is going to mean promotion for you if you get this delivered."

In high spirits Chip set off on his errand.

In the Fire Station yard El Dragon watched one of the men focussing the sunlight on a piece of wood by means of the remains of a broken bottle.

"What are you doing?" asked El Dragon.

"Making a fire," replied the man. "It is easier this way than rubbing two pieces of sticks together."

"Are you going to do some cooking?" El Dragon enquired.

"No, just a celebration."

El Dragon did not like to ask too many questions. He was rapidly learning the wisdom of accumulating information by observation.

As time went on quite a crowd began to gather and he wondered vaguely where all the Party men could be to allow so many people to assemble together. Surely it was not in the interests of the Republic to let so many malcontents congregate. He would put a stop to this sort of thing when he resumed power. Then the consoling thought struck him that very soon his message would be examined at headquarters. Soon the Party men would come to his rescue and the Revolutionaries would be caught red-handed.

Chapter 10.

Chip arrived at Headquarters with his precious package and was checked at the door by an array of spears and pikes. "What do you want?" demanded an officer, drawing his sword.

"I have a message for the Chief," replied Chip.

"Who from?" asked the officer.

"From El Dragon."

The Officer scowled. "Stop being funny," he warned. "We've got more important things to do than have little jokes with riffraffs like you. Now clear out, quick."

"But please, officer, this is a written message," and he hastily unwrapped the banana leaf. "Look!"

The Officer hesitated, then called to one of the guards. "Here, put this man in the Guard Room," and taking the package he vanished into the building.

It was quite a while before the Chief was ready to see him, then the clay was placed on the desk and together they studied the message.

"It is obviously a hoax," declared the Officer. "Somebody is trying to make us look foolish. Look at the date — April 1st. Just imagine what it would be like if we made elaborate preparations to welcome visitors and then for us to wait all day and nobody comes. We would never be able to live it down."

But the Chief was not so sure. The message was in capital letters but the signature was in handwriting and might possibly be that of El Dragon himself, absurd though it seemed that he could have got back into the country without the knowledge of the Party. He ordered an immediate meeting of the Council.

The Council gathered around the table and examined the message closely. It was quite obvious that they were somewhat disturbed.

"Comrades," said the Chief, calling them to order. "There are several things we have got to decide. First, is this authentic? If so, what are we going to do about El Dragon and what are we going to do about the Great Ally and the danger to the Party. Second, if we cannot decide whether it is authentic or not, what precautions must we take to safeguard ourselves in case it is true. Should we prepare a welcome?"

"It is a very awkward situation," agreed one, "but authentic or not, I think we should be very cautious about any extensive celebrations of welcome or we'll have people scratching up notices: 'Ally, go home' or something like that. No, I think we had better make no preparations at all and pretend to know nothing about it. In all probability it is a hoax as the officer suggests."

"That is all very well," agreed the Chief. "But this signature looks remarkably like that of El Dragon."

"But that could easily have been forged," pointed out another.

"Just a minute," said the Chief of the Investigation Department.

I have just remembered something. I was this morning investigating the outbreak of prisoners from the Depository and outside the building I found an empty box that I have not seen before. And now that I come to think about it I believe I remember seeing El Dragon's name on it, and I think I remember seeing the stamp of the Great Ally on the box, too."

The Council was astounded. "Is El Dragon really back in the country?" they wondered.

"We had better call in the caretaker of the Depository at once," said the Chief, "and get him to explain the box."

The caretaker was sent for and the Chief went on. "This is getting very serious. Now, supposing El Dragon really is here then what can he mean by saying he is a prisoner? Why should he be a prisoner? And what does he mean by the Fire Station. There aren't any Fire Stations now since we ran out of buckets."

"Perhaps he means one of the former Fire Stations," suggested one.

"Yes, that may be it," agreed the Chief. "But the question is, if El Dragon really is in the country, if he really is a prisoner in one of the old fire stations, what are we going to do about him? Should we rescue him?"

It seemed to be quite a delicate point and the men seemed reluctant to answer. Nobody spoke for a while. Then someone put forward the useful suggestion, "Well, at any rate we can find out if there is a plot against the Party."

At this point the caretaker was ushered in, obviously very nervous.

The Chief of the Investigation Department interrogated him and came to the point at once. "We want a full explanation of the box we found outside the Depository."

The Caretaker decided it was best to tell the truth. "It was a fella trying to smuggle in a case of cups and saucers, pretending to be El Dragon."

"Did you trouble to notice that the case bore his name and the stamp of the Great Ally?"

"Well, anyone can mark cases if they have the proper paint and things."

"I see. So you didn't think it necessary to seek a higher opinion than your own? It did not occur to you that we might be interested in those cases."

The caretaker hung his head and trembled.

"Just a moment," interjected the Chief. "What was this man wearing?"

"He was wearing a pair of dark blue trousers with a red and white stripe," replied the caretaker.

"There you are," cried the Chief, banging the table with his fist. "That must be him. That is the pair of trousers I lent him when he left the Republic. Nobody else in the country has a pair like them. This is more serious than we thought. This is a genuine message. We have got to move very cautiously, comrades. What I suggest is this. We must send two reliable Party men to each Fire Station to see if there is anything unusual going on there and report back here as soon as they have anything definite one way or the other. Tell them they are to locate a man in blue pants with a red and white stripe. That should not be a difficult task. The trousers will make him quite conspicuous. Comrades, stand by to be instantly recalled." Then, turning to the Minister of Defence, "Make sure you have all your men properly prepared for action. This is a state of emergency. Comrades, the meeting is adjourned."

In the Fire Station yard a fire was burning merrily and a large crowd had gathered. The Leaders of the Rebels were addressing the People in turn. They reminded their listeners of the poverty of the People and the wealth of the lazy Party men — "these parasites who sweat the guts out of us and bleed us to death so that they can live in luxury. We have put up with it long enough." (Cheers from the assembled crowd). "The People must rise and get rid of the Government." (Cheers). "Down with the Government."

Someone produced the Republic flag. The Leaders grasped it firmly in their hands and tore it to pieces and trampled it in the dust amid frantic cheers from the People. Then, with great ceremony they threw the remnants into the flames.

"And now, friends," said the old man when he had at last quietened the People, "I introduce to you Fitz, our Leader, who in a few days will liberate the country with the help of his friends from overseas." Another wave of cheering broke out as El Dragon stepped before the enthusiastic crowd. Someone had unearthed from somewhere the old flag of the Imperialist Power and draped it solemnly around his shoulders. "Kiss it," whispered the old man.

El Dragon was in a desperate position. It seemed that he had no alternative. There was no sign of a rescue party. Chips had not returned. Slowly he raised the corner of the Imperialist flag to his lips and the cheering began again.

"Friends," he began, "This is a momentous moment. I have come to help you. Help is coming from across the seas—"

The two Party spies who had been looking on waited for no more. They hastened back to Headquarters to report. They had seen and heard enough.

Chapter 11.

The members of the council were perplexed. They were faced with a revolution.

"The question is," commented the Chief, "Just how El Dragon intends to move. What is behind the message? That is what I cannot understand. Why should he tell us where he is and issue a warning? It doesn't seem to make sense to start a Revolution and then to tell us just where we can find him."

"It was a trap," declared the Minister of Defence. "Probably the whole place is full of guns that he has smuggled in on the quiet. Probably that was what was in the packing case."

"But the caretaker says it was cups and saucers."

"That was the tale the caretaker told," persisted the Defence Minister. "Probably El Dragon gave him some cups and saucer, to keep quiet about the guns. Remember," he added significantly, "We have seen nothing of the Depository Guards ever since he arrived."

"That's true," commented several.

"Well, then", the Defence Minister went on, "What I suggest is this: El Dragon never went to the Great Ally at all. Instead, he negotiated with the Imperialist Power, arranged for arms to be smuggled into the Republic and then came back to stir up the People in revolt and set himself up as Dictator."

"Shame!" cried the members of the Council.

"Now he feels so sure of himself," the Defence Minister continued, "that he tried to lure us into a trap at the Fire Station. The mention of April 1st was just a phrase to make it sound authentic. What I propose to do is to send an armed force to each Fire Station except the one where we know he is. Then they will believe that we have been taken in by his note and are visiting the Fire Stations systematically in an effort to rescue him. Then they will not know that we realise the truth."

"But how will you deal with the uprising?" enquired the Chief.

"Ah, I have thought of that. We will have a close watch kept on the Fire Station and on all gatherings of the People and whenever opportunities arise we will round up all suspects. The night before April 1st. we will set fire to the Fire Station and during the hours of darkness we will sink some of our oldest boats across the river to prevent any shipping coming in, in case there should be any truth in that part of the message."

"Just a minute," interrupted the Chief who had been examining the clay message very closely. "I wonder if there is not a different meaning altogether. Perhaps this message was not meant to get into our hands at all. Let us suppose it was intended for the chief of his confederates somewhere in the town. 'Ally from across the seas arrives April 1st' might be just a code phrase for foreign aid. 'Plot against Party' may be an instruction to commence stirring up the People in anticipation of an invasion. He wrote 'imprisoned' because at that time he was imprisoned – in the Depository and therefore had to explain why he was not delivering his message personally. 'Fire Station' may be a further instruction – to set fire to the Railway Station – perhaps some prearranged signal."

It was all very bewildering.

"Well," said the Defence Minister, my plan seems to be a good one either way. We can have a watch kept on the Railway Station and I would also suggest that we send all available gold and diamonds to Vascalia and Bombador to purchase arms. There is just time for us to get a supply by April 1st."

The Council agreed and authorised the Defence Minister to put the country in a state of alert. If El Dragon wanted to make war, he should have it!

Chapter 12.

It was March 31st. Party men had ordered the People to decorate the streets and had been amazed at the readiness of the People. The Rebel Leaders were frankly puzzled. Why should The Party be making preparations? Had they got wind of the coming invasion and were preparing to capitulate? But it could scarcely be that, for they had noted certain military preparations that had been going on for days. It was known that the Members of the Council had all been trying on their suits of armour. The rebels had changed their headquarters as soon as they learned of the Party visits to other fire stations. They were now back in the Depository.

They decided to consult El Dragon. They found him sitting dejectedly in a corner wearing the Imperialist flag as a cloak over his shoulders. The Leaders had insisted that he should wear this as his badge of office. "Look here, Fitz," the old man said. "Are you sure everything is going to be all right for tomorrow? Are you sure your friends will come?"

"Quite sure," replied El Dragon, but he had an awful sinking feeling in his stomach. Supposing no one came! He would be in a terrible mess.

"How many warships will be coming?" persisted one.

"Quite sufficient, you may be sure of that," replied El Dragon.

"And what about aircraft and land forces?" asked another.

"I cannot give you precise details. The important thing is that I must be on the spot when they arrive. What I expected to happen is that a boat will come with a small party of civilians who will claim to be tourists. In actual fact they will be here to contact me. The others will come later. Just get me in a position where I can step forward to greet them."

The leaders did not seem altogether satisfied.

About midday a plane flew low over the Capital. Every eye in the city gazed up. There was great excitement everywhere. This seemed to be a signal. People everywhere talked about it. What puzzled many was that it had been identified as a Vascalian plane.

Late in the afternoon excitement broke out afresh when another plane flew low over the town. This plane had the markings of Bombador. "False markings," was the conclusion reached by many.

The Rebel Leaders made their dispositions and gave their final instructions, "— and remember, do nothing until you see Fitz shake hands with the visitors and hand over a bouquet of flowers."

The sun sank and a nervous tension settled over the entire city and the surrounding countryside. All through the hours of darkness thousands began to converge on the Capital. Nobody thought of sleep that night. Tomorrow was April 1st.

El Dragon was getting desperate. Somehow he must warn the Party. His chance came unexpectedly just after midnight.

He had stopped for a moment at the door of the Depository, at the very moment that the guards were called in for briefing. The coast was clear. There appeared to be nobody in sight. He ran as fast as he could go.

By great good fortune he had not been noticed. At last he was free. There was still time to save the Republic.

Breathlessly he arrived at the grounds in which stood the Party Headquarters. A nervous guard, hearing the sound of rapid footsteps, fired his revolver. El Dragon had to take cover and lost his cloak in the process. This was terrible.

The shot had put everyone on the alert. People in their houses wondered if the revolt had actually started, for was it not past midnight? Was it not April 1st. already?

At the same moment, the Rebel Leaders discovered that Fitz was missing, and there was consternation in the Depository. After a hurried consultation, it was decided that whatever the circumstances the People must not know that their appointed leader was missing. They must pretend that all was going according to plan.

If he could not be found, then someone must impersonate him.

"We will have to get a pair of trousers from somewhere, then," shrewdly observed one.

"You are quite right," agreed the old man. "The only places where you are likely to get any are in the houses of Party men.

Send a search party out at once for a pair of trousers as near as you can to the right colour. Dark blue with a red and white stripe."

A consultation was also in progress at Party headquarters.

An officer was anxiously asking the guard what had happened.

"I was standing just outside the front entrance when I heard the sound of men rushing towards me —" the guard began.

"How many?" asked the officer.

"I should say about fifty," replied the guard.

"And what did you do?"

"I fired at the first and they all ran for cover."

"Good work, Comrade" complimented the officer. "Now, you say about fifty?" He tapped the desk with his fingers. "If fifty were rushing the building, there must be a lot more about. It is most probable that we are surrounded. Comrades, put up the barricades. We are besieged by the rebels."

Hastily the Party men set to work barricading the windows and doors.

Meanwhile the rebel search party had gladly set off on their quest for trousers. Most of them selected houses of some notorious Party men, but there were three who decided to be bolder. They decided to go direct to Party Headquarters.

As they drew near to the building they became more cautious.

There was tension in the air. Anything could happen.

Silently they crept forward and were puzzled at the sounds of hammering going on inside the building. They noticed that all the windows were closed, and shuttered.

That was going to make things awkward. It seemed that they had made a mistake. They should have gone to one of the private houses after all.

Suddenly they came to a halt. No, they were in luck. There, with his back towards them, pressed close against a tree was a man wearing dark trousers.

Silently they crept forward. Then at a signal from the leader they sprang. One put his hand over the victim's mouth, another grasped his arms. In a few moments their task was accomplished and they returned triumphant to the rebel headquarters.

"Good work, boys," congratulated the old man. "This is the very thing. Nobody will be able to tell the difference."

Crouching behind the tree outside the Party Headquarters, El Dragon was almost in tears. Furtively, he reached out for the Imperialist flag and draped it around his shivering body. He thought he deserved better of the country he was trying to save.

Somewhere in the town a big fire was raging. El Dragon became more anxious. Perhaps some of those irresponsible rebels had begun sabotage already. It was desperately urgent for him to reach the members of the Council.

Slowly, inch-by-inch he crawled forward till he was within ten or twelve yards of the building. Everything seemed very quiet now. The hammering had stopped. He raised himself to one knee in order to obtain a better view. He heard a swishing noise and then saw an arrow quivering in the ground beside him.

He slithered quickly away.

What should he do? Obviously they had no idea who he was. He decided that he had better try calling to them. "Hello, there," he called. "This is El Dragon. Let me in." A shower of arrows was the only response to his call. He was glad at least they were conserving their ammunition.

A few minutes later he heard the sound of approaching footsteps. He decided to wait and see what was going to happen.

Unaware of the situation, the group of men came on rapidly only to be greeted by a shower of arrows.

Astounded, they took cover. "Hey, we are Party men," they shouted.

Another shower of arrows showed that the defenders did not believe them.

"We are reporting that we have just set fire to the Fire Station," explained one.

There was a hurried consultation within. "Send one member forward slowly until we say halt. If anyone else moves we will use our guns."

Very nervously one walked forward until he was halted about five yards from the entrance. "Give your name, Party number, name of your immediate superior officer and your last consignment before this."

The man gave the required particulars. There was a pause during which it was obvious that facts were being checked, then the door was cautiously opened and he was permitted to enter. A few more minutes and the O.K. was given to the rest of the party to proceed.

It was the opportunity El Dragon had been awaiting. Attaching himself to the rear of the group he passed safely inside the building and was greatly relieved to hear the sound of the doors being barred behind him. He had to admit to himself that although he had been fired upon he was secretly glad that the Party was proving to be realistic.

Home again! Back in the midst of his Party friends! Now all was going to be well. He pushed his way forward, his hand out-stretched, "Well done, comrades."

The men were shocked to see in their midst the stranger wrapped in the Imperialist flag. This was absolutely the last word in insults. Without hesitation they tied him up and threw him in a corner. "But let me explain," expostulated El Dragon.

"Shut up," commanded one of the captors.

El Dragon sat listening to the conversation and was relieved to know that it had been the Party men who had started the fire. Perhaps things were not as bad as he had thought. No Council members were about so he decided to wait. It was very hot in the building with all the windows boarded up. The sound of voices seemed to become a monotonous drone. El Dragon slept.

Chapter 13.

April 1st had dawned. The population of the city seemed to have grown to four times its normal size. Crowds lined the shore looking steadfastly out to sea.

The buildings were decorated with leaves and flowers, and everywhere there was an atmosphere of excited anticipation.

The members of the Council were, with the exception of the Minister of Defence, in an angry mood. They had all awakened to find their trousers stolen. It was a very strangely arrayed Council that met early that morning.

El Dragon had several times called out to the guards since waking but they had become so tired of trying to silence him that he was now gagged. Being short of cloth they had filled his mouth with the clay he had written his message on. They had then put him in the guardroom.

After a few minutes he realised that he was not alone. In another corner sat the dejected figure of his recent messenger Chip. "Boss," Chip exclaimed when the guards had left the room, "However did you get caught? What's going wrong?"

El Dragon groaned and realising his plight Chip crossed the room and began to unloose the ropes. At last El Dragon was free and able to remove the mud from his mouth. Whatever could he tell Chip? What could be done?

"Look, Chip. We have got to get out of here quick," said El Dragon.

"Sure, Boss, but how?"

"There must be some way."

"I have been here for days and haven't found a way out yet. What day is it today?"

"April 1st."

El Dragon groaned and buried his head in his hands. "Then it is the Day of Liberation!"

"Cheer up, Boss," said Chip. "We will soon get rid of the Party and then you will be free."

They could hear the sound of crowds gathering in the streets. El Dragon began to think furiously. If it was impossible to break out, then he must attract the attention of the People to try to get them to come to his aid. Then he had a brainwave. The flag! The Imperialist Flag! In a matter of seconds he had thrust it through the bars of the window and was waving it frantically.

Someone in the crowd saw it and a cheer was raised. The flag! The old flag! And waving from the Republic Headquarters!

The People could hardly believe their eyes. They cheered and cheered, but walked on. The situation seemed hopeless. How could he make people understand?

To make matters worse, a Party man passing by noticed it and came in hurriedly to investigate. There was a tramp of feet and a key turned in the lock.

It was at this moment that a plane was heard approaching the city.

The Defence Minister handled the situation remarkably well. He did not quite know what was about to happen but at least it did not seem that there was going to be an immediate large-scale invasion. Perhaps this plane brought an ultimatum.

He decided to treat this as a local skirmish and planned accordingly. He trained his rifles on the road leading from the ramp where the plane was going to land, and set his archers and pikemen to deal with any disturbance in the crowd. He was somewhat uneasy however to learn that no reinforcements had come in from the provinces. Perhaps it was as he had suggested at one of the Council meetings.

This was a feint while an invasion had begun elsewhere. If so, then it was strange that so many people had come into town. However, one task at a time. It seemed that at least he had this situation well in hand.

As Fitz had not arrived, the Rebel Leaders had at last appointed the representative who was to wear the trousers. But they had not bargained for the careful planning of the Defence Minister. They had not expected that the Party would have been making plans for a reception. Someone must have betrayed them. They were puzzled by the disappearance first of Chip and then of Fitz. However, they must just await the right moment. The man with the trousers lingered inconspicuously at the back of the crowd carrying his bouquet of flowers.

Meanwhile at the Party headquarters all the men had rushed out at the sight of the plane. El Dragon and Chip seized their opportunity to escape through the unlocked door, delaying only sufficiently long for the former to wind securely about him the Imperialist flag which now meant so much to him.

Poppemoff, Kopit and Clod stared through the windows as the plane skimmed across the water to the ramp. "Why this is wonderful," said Kopit. "I had never expected such an enthusiastic welcome. Just look at the crowds."

"A military display too." said Poppemoff.

"Look at the flowers," added Clod. "This is a new experience."

Smiling happily the three visitors waited for the plane to stop.

Everybody had, of course, by this time noticed that the plane bore the markings of the Great Ally but both Party men and Rebels were unanimous in the belief that they were false markings.

Chapter 14.

Poppemoff, Kopit and Clod stepped from the plane and stood for a moment in the hot sunshine. It was very strange, they thought, that no officials had come forward to meet them. Most unusual! The menacing guns made them feel uncomfortable though the cheering of the crowds kept their spirits up.

"Very queer!" commented Clod.

"Very!" agreed Poppemoff.

"I say, an idea has just struck me," said Kopit. "Do you know what today is? Well, it is April 1st, and all those countries which have the old Imperialist tradition make a joke of everything and everybody on that day. They try to catch everybody out and that sort of thing."

"Oh," said Poppemoff and Clod, somewhat relieved.

"Yes, let us enter into the spirit of it," suggested Kopit, "Come on."

The three strode forward. The riflemen seemed more menacing than ever. "Ha, ha, ha," laughed the visitors, "You can't fool us."

Kopit pointed to an imaginary aeroplane in the sky, Clod to an imaginary submarine in the river and while the gaze of the startled riflemen was diverted the visitors walked through their ranks. "Ha, ha, ha," they shrieked, slapping a sergeant on the back. "You can't trick us," and the crowd roared their approval.

Then Clod noticed the archers and pikemen. "I say," he exclaimed, "Just look at that. They have put on a historical pageant for our benefit. My word, this is wonderful."

"And look at those chaps in medieval armour," said Kopit spotting the Ministers standing in a nervous group further down the road. We must get them to put on a contest for us with battle-axes."

"Never seen anything like it," agreed Poppemoff. "This is simply marvellous. Blinkersov gave us no idea that we would find such a happy, contented people."

The riflemen, having overcome their momentary lapse closed in behind the advancing visitors.

El Dragon wrung his hand in exasperation. Whatever was going to happen? Why should the Council and the Party men be treating the representatives of the Great Ally in such a threatening manner?

Blocking his way were ranks of riflemen, pikemen, and archers. And there in the distance, surrounded by the Party men all donned in heavy suits of armour, was a man holding a bouquet of flowers.

"And he is wearing my trousers! The ones with the stripes down the side!" cried El Dragon despairingly, not sure what to do next.

Somehow, that man must be prevented from reaching the visitors for if that bouquet was presented, the Revolution would begin. El Dragon was the only man who could do anything.

Without hesitation, he barged through the military ranks and dashed after the advancing figure of the man carrying the flowers. With a spectacular rugby tackle El Dragon threw him to the ground.

"Just look at this," said Kopit delightedly. "They are putting on an all-in wrestling match for us as well."

"Why is that fellow wearing the Imperialist flag?" asked Poppemoff thoughtfully.

"Ah, that is probably one of the customs of the Republic. It is probably intended that he should lose the fight in order to please us," suggested Clod.

"But he seems to be winning," pointed out Kopit.

"In that case," said Poppemoff proudly, "One of us had better take him on for the honour of our country. We must not allow the Imperialist flag to win."

El Dragon at last succeeded in overcoming his opponent knocking his head on the ground to make sure that he was unconscious. He had succeeded in preventing the presentation of the bouquet that would have fired the revolution.

Now, panting, dishevelled but elated, the moment had come to whisper a message to the visitors that would save the whole situation.

To his amazement, he saw that Clod had removed his jacket and was about to spring upon him. There was no time for any sort of message. A grim struggle was thrust upon him.

It was a terrible situation to be in: in full view of the People, to be fighting a guest he had invited. He dared not lose lest the fatal handshake and bouquet presentation take place. Breathing heavily, he closed with his opponent and rolled over and over in the dust.

"I'm El Dragon," he whispered into Clod's ear.

"That may be," came the quick reply, "and I am Clod," and gave him a vicious uppercut that made El Dragon see stars. Grimly he held on. He realised, from the power of the blows he was receiving, that Clod was taking the matter seriously. El Dragon also realised that he must win this fight too. He twisted and kicked and punched as the occasion demanded till at last a lucky blow caught Clod plumb on the chin and he rolled over unconscious. He had won round two for the Republic!

When he stood up he noticed that Kopit had already removed his jacket.

It was a good thing that the active life of recent months had made him very fit. He did not flinch as Kopit approached him waving his arms menacingly. He could see that the man was deeply offended, that Clod, a guest, had been so roughly treated. But what else could he do? He began to wish he had not condemned religion so heartily in recent years. A prayer might have sustained him at this crisis. He noticed that the crowd was no longer cheering.

The next moment, Kopit was upon him with flailing fists and he was hard put to it to keep clear.

Kopit was a hard hitter as El Dragon quickly found. In a few minutes he was decidedly getting the worst of it. An eye was closing and his nose was bleeding.

He set his teeth and waded into that windmill of flailing fists. By the greatest of good fortune he caught Kopit off-balance and had the satisfaction of seeing him fall to the ground. This would give him a breathing space, if only for a moment, El Dragon thought.

But to his horror, he noticed out of the corner of his eye that the man in the trousers was beginning to get up and was reaching out for the bouquet of flowers lying in the road. "Merciful God," prayed El Dragon, "give me strength," and just had time to kick the flowers further down the road before Kopit was on him again.

With great presence of mind he sidestepped, and, thrusting a foot out-tripped his antagonist who went sprawling on top of the flowers.

The man in the borrowed trousers, still dazed, but dimly aware that he must get hold of the flowers lunged at the prostrate Kopit and they rolled over together punching frantically.

At last, Kopit got on top and with a final blow knocked the man unconscious again.

He rose panting to his feet. El Dragon had had the breathing space he needed. With a right to the stomach and a left to the jaw, Kopit had had it, too.

Wearily El Dragon turned. Poppemoff was waiting for him.

Poppemoff was well over six feet tall. Poppemoff was enraged and El Dragon quailed at the murderous look he saw in his opponent's eyes. Poppemoff looked strong and fresh. El Dragon felt weak at the knees. His arms ached. His head ached. He felt sore all over.

Then Poppemoff was upon him. Blows rained thick and fast seemingly everywhere at once. They thudded upon his body and smashed into his face and he began to feel that he no longer cared what happened. Anything to get away from this terrible monster. Another heavy blow and he fell to the ground. Something strange seemed to be happening to the world around him. The crowd and the buildings all seemed to be swaying backwards and forwards. He felt so weary. He would like to sleep and sleep.

Then he became aware of a second figure standing beside him, a figure he could dimly see was holding a bouquet of flowers. "Oh, dear God," he prayed. "Give me strength and I promise to go to Church for the rest of my life." With a last desperate effort he jerked to his feet. His head came into contact with Poppemoff's chin. He swung his aim wildly and caught his opponent's ear as he swayed from the impact. He had sufficient presence of mind to realise his advantage and struck again and finally with all his remaining strength he hit his opponent over the heart.

Poppemoff fell to the ground and lay motionless. El Dragon was conscious of someone presenting him with the bouquet and then he too fell down and thereafter remembered no more.

The crowds had dispersed, bewildered.

The Party men stood about in groups, bewildered.

The Members of the Council assembled at Headquarters, bewildered.

Poppemoff, Kopit and Clod, sore and angry sat in the guardroom, bewildered.

El Dragon was just being revived and having his wounds dressed. His body seemed to be one huge ache. His feet felt heavy as lead. It hurt him to move. His knuckles were sore and raw. He could hardly see out of his eyes, his face was bruised all over, and the skin split in many places. But inside he was elated. It had been a glorious victory. Single-handedly he had saved the Republic.

While he was recovering in another room, the member of the Council spoke reverently of him as 'Hero of the Republic'.

The Council was in session and the Chief was speaking. "What we have got to find out is what country these three have come from. What I cannot understand is why there are only three of them."

"I still think," said the Defence Minister, "That it had all been a bluff to cover up something else in the Republic."

"We had better have them brought in to give an account of themselves," suggested another.

And so the three foreign captives were brought before them, more enraged than ever.

"Your names and the reason for your coming?" demanded the Chief, rather nervously.

Poppemoff acted as spokesman and with great dignity announced their names and status as officials of the Great Ally, then demanded to see El Dragon.

"El Dragon?" said the Chief and began to have some misgivings—could it be—?

He asked the visitors to retire. Hurriedly he discussed his fears with the other members of the Council. Perhaps there had been some mistake. Perhaps El Dragon was in the country after all.

Instructions were given for the 'Hero of the Republic' to be brought in. Perhaps he could throw light on the problem.

El Dragon was brought in on a crude stretcher. He waved feebly to the Council and tried to smile but found that it hurt his split lip.

"Who are you?" asked the Chief.

"El Dragon," came the weary reply.

"El Dragon!" came the amazed chorus.

"Where are my friends?" asked El Dragon.

"Your friends?" The Council was puzzled.

"Yes, the friends I fought," explained El Dragon, though it hurt him to speak.

The three men were re-called amid general embarrassment and introduced to El Dragon. Then the story began to unfold.

"Then there was no revolution at all!" the Chief declared.

"It will go down as the greatest April 1st joke in history," groaned the Minister of Defence.

There was a rap on the door of the Council chamber. An orderly entered breathlessly. "Chief," he said. "We have been invaded."

"What!" Everybody stood up except El Dragon who could not.

"Who by?"

"The Vascalians crossed the frontier this morning at dawn."

Everybody was dumbfounded. Another doubt began to appear in their minds. – Perhaps El Dragon and the three visitors were part of a bigger plot.

The situation was tense. There seemed nothing they could do except capitulate. Dismally they discussed the situation.

Then came another rap on the door. Another breathless orderly appeared. "Chief" he said, "Bombador has begun to invade us".

This was the last straw. "To whom must we capitulate?" asked the Chief in bewilderment.

El Dragon smiled. "Perhaps the best thing we can do is to ask the Imperialist Power to help," and he lifted the tattered fragments of his flag.

THE END

Afterword

We do not know what response this novel generated in British Guiana. That the *Daily Argosy* was willing to publish it, and devote a sizeable amount of space to it, indicates it must have been pertinent at the time in addressing a wound that was opening in the national politics.

1. The Fear of the White Man Caught in the Sidelines

In choosing a pseudonym to write this novel, our father had a genuine fear of reprisals. This is an extract from a letter he wrote in 1953 to his UK supervisor, a Mr Calder of the Colonial Missionary Society.

Now a word about the situation here. You will recall that a long time back I wrote that there was evidence of a certain feeling against Whites. This has grown in recent months as a result of increasing political ferment. The

P.P.P. (People's Progressive Party) was swept into power with such a large majority that they had a free hand to do almost as they liked. They have used their power in an alarming manner. It became obvious weeks ago that the leaders were determined by any methods to cripple the 'foreign' industries and to educate the people along communistic lines, threatening to take the schools away from the churches and educate the children politically. Time and again they boasted that if they did not get their own way they would use force. Incidents of rowdyism began to occur, opponents of P.P.P. were stoned at meetings, a Catholic priest was roughly handled. While at Bartica I heard a group of men say, "Within a few months all the Whites in the colony will be gone." Some missionaries have been considering evacuating their families.

It was while I was at Bartica I got the idea of writing a story in a farcical vein depicting what would happen in a country of this size if, in fact, independence should be obtained and foreign capital and equipment withdrawn. I hoped that in its subtlety it would get the ordinary people to 'think'.

You will be interested to know that during the past week it has been running as a serial in The Daily Argosy. Despite the pressure of sensational news and the fact that the paper has only six or eight pages the editor has devoted half or three-quarters of a page to the story, daily.

I should add, that at his advice the name Mathieson was used. Perhaps he was afraid my house would be burnt down!

Subsequent events have given source for alarm. It has been noticeable in the past two weeks-or-so how the P.P.P. leaders were saying outrageous things with a marked note of confidence. Evidence of incendiarism began to appear.

Police on many occasions showed an unwillingness to interfere. I heard reports of some people who had been threatened. It became more and more obvious that trouble was brewing. A few days ago I heard confidentially that large quantities of fuel were being bought by P.P.P. men. The sale of guns and ammunition last weekend reached surprising proportions. (Gunpowder is sold without licence.)

This, as briefly as I can put it, is something of what has led to the tense situation at the moment.

On the surface all is quiet but one might almost say too quiet. An inter-colonial test cricket match which began today had only a few hundred spectators as against the usual thousands. Guards are stationed at all strategic points, including newspaper offices. Meetings at night of more than five people are banned. Certain prominent people are under threat because of anti-P.P.P. attitude. We are having suitcases ready-packed in case it is necessary to evacuate the family.

Personally I doubt there will be any trouble, but should anything serious happen, here is the address of my wife's family (...and he inserted an address near Tunbridge Wells, Kent, in the United Kingdom).

George Musgrave

It is clear that although George was never actually threatened physically, yet he was aware of a pervasive attitude of resentment causing him to be concerned for his life and the life of his family. He wrote in his biography *A Speck of Dust* how someone on a pushbike swerved across the road to swear at him, "Clear out of our country." He heard about the statue of Queen Victoria being blown up in the city centre. And he saw the graffiti on walls, "*Limeys Out!*"

2. Cheddi Jagan and the People's Progressive Party

In 1953, the United Kingdom were the colonial rulers of British Guiana, with The Queen as Head of State, and a Governor posted in the capital city, Georgetown. Yet the nation had a democratically-elected parliament that saw to the day-to-day running of the country.

Gradual tensions and unrest in the country resulted in the People's Progressive Party (the P.P.P.) winning the election in April 1953. It was a landslide victory, led by their leader Cheddi Jagan, winning two-thirds of the seats in Parliament.

Cheddi Jagan appeared as a champion of the people, a man campaigning for worker's rights, for union representation for labourers on the sugar cane plantations in Demarara, and for the bauxite workers. Ultimately he campaigned for independence from the Imperialistic British. He had led a series of strikes and encouraged civilian unrest.

Cheddi Jagan had an Asian background (his father was an Indian immigrant), and Cheddi was married to a White American woman from Chicago, Janet Rosenberg. Such a mixed-race marriage ought to have been seen as beneficial to the country, but the colonial rulers did not see it that way. It was feared that Cheddi Jagan believed in a Marxist philosophy. Next to fascism, this was seemingly an unforgivable sin in the eyes of post-war Britain and America.

In October 1953, fearing Jagan was steering his country towards Communism, the British suspended the Guianese constitution and sent in troops to quash any anarchistic uprising.

In an affront to Democracy, the British dismissed the House of Assembly and the Government Ministers and several members of the P.P.P. were arrested. Civil rights were suspended. In their place, they reinstated members of the opposition into government positions, from the party that had lost the election! All this, under the signature of Winston Churchill (the British Prime Minister), and of the young monarch, Queen Elizabeth II, in her inaugural first year's reign on the throne.

Such was the fear of Communism, the British were willing to hypocritically suspend Democracy. No wonder it was considered a *coup d'etat* against the elected government.

Churchill sent hundreds of troops to secure strategic sites, stationed the warship *HMS Superb* off the coast, and sent frigates up the Essiquibo. That'll subdue them!

Yet when the British troops arrived on 9th October 1953 they were surprised to find the streets peaceful, and everyone going about their normal business.

Nevertheless, the Jagans were arrested, and Parliament disbanded.

The British evidently had believed the fake news that was being peddled across the oceans. Perhaps G H Mathieson's little spoof novel had already stirred up a hornet's nest in Westminster.

Concern at Cheddi Jagan's beliefs sparked the British MI5 into action. They had his and his wife Janet's communications tapped. In fact for over a decade their letters were intercepted, phones tapped, and they were kept under physical surveillance. The Americans, too, didn't want another Socialist State on their doorstep – they already had Cuba too close for comfort.

But was this *coup* really staged for ideological reasons? Or were the British fearful they were losing their control of a cheap supply of sugar cane and of bauxite – between them 90% of Guiana's exports – and of an accessible good source of hardwood timber? Placer deposits of gold were also becoming profitably extracted. The British wouldn't want to lose access to such a lucrative source of commodities.

But Jagan's premise was that these riches were been extracted while the Guianese people were being exploited in a land that 'endured squalor and poverty with a long glaring contrast between rich and poor' in dilapidated communities that 'lacked every amenity and frequently surrounded by stagnant water' (*The Manchester Guardian, 1953*). Jagan sought to improve these 'dreadful housing and social conditions' and that is why he was elected to office. He sought to improve health services, impose a minimum wage and promote Trade Unions.

While Jagan's motives were good, his proposals to redistribute wealth into the hands of the workforce went against the expectations of the British Government.

So when the P.P.P. called for strikes in the August of 1953, and sugar production subsequently ground to a halt causing ladies in English tea-rooms in the Savoy and on Bexhill seafront to restrict the number of sugar lumps with their Earl Grey, the British realised some drastic action had to be taken. Perhaps this was Guiana's version of the Boston Tea Party! Send in the troops so we can have sugar in our tea.

As a result of all this, five leading members of the P.P.P. were interned on the 27th October 1953, and in the following April Cheddi Jagan was given a six-month prison sentence. Presumably their crimes were plotting a *coup*, just like the British Government themselves had performed!

On his release, his movements were restricted, and he was confined to the capital city, Georgetown. In the early 1960s he did get elected to lead his country once again, for a brief period (1961-1964).

Despite the antagonism of the British, there is no actual evidence that Jagan had any ties to foreign communist or revolutionary groups. It was a trend, instigated by US Senator McCarthy during the Cold War 'witch hunts', to falsely label certain politicians as a Marxist when all they were trying to do is raise their compatriots off the bottom rung of abject poverty. And Cheddi Jagan had been similarly accused. Even so, the possibility had sparked a British military intervention within a few months of his victory.

George Musgrave got to know both sides of the political establishment during his short tenure as church minister in Georgetown (1950-1954). He was regularly invited to the luxurious grounds of the British Ambassador's residence. And he knew Cheddi Jagan, too. It was Cheddi who waved George off at the airport when he finally returned to England in 1954, and Cheddi was the last person in Guiana to shake his hand. My father fondly spoke of this final departure. Whether for Cheddi it was a suppressed good-riddance we will never know.

3. The PNC Party: Forbes Burnham and Independence.

Forbes Burnham had been a member of the P.P.P. alongside Cheddi Jagan. He had been appointed as Minister for Education in Jagan's first cabinet. He was of Afro-Guianese descent, and born in Georgetown. But seemingly he did not share as vociferously the alleged Marxist views held by Jagan. Consequently, both the British and Americans looked favourably upon him as a future Prime Minister. Burnham realised the current political climate called for a less Socialist stance so that in 1955 he split from the P.P.P. raising his own party, the *People's National Congress* (P.N.C.).

Despite Cheddi Jagan's P.P.P. being the most popular party, Burnham's P.N.C. formed a coalition with the *United Force* party, thus winning successive elections, and the British and Americans were keen to keep him in power to pursue moderate policies.

When, on 26 May 1966, Guyana became an independent country, Burnham was at the helm, supposedly steadying the ship, with his pro-western policies.

But as with so many Premiers in charge of newly emerging nations, the desire for more ultimate power seemed irresistible. Police were given powers to crush opposition. Electoral irregularities became suspicious. Mysteriously his party achieved over 90% of the vote. The unmentionable word 'corruption' reared its ugly head. Ties were formed with communist states such as Russia, Cuba, and North Korea. Industries were nationalised and imports strictly controlled. As everyone feared, Guyana had become a Socialist State.

It was not until after Burnham's death in 1985 that America became more involved in ensuring free and fair elections, implemented by Jimmy Carter. Ironically, it was Cheddi Jagan who again won the national vote, and he became President in 1992 until his death in 1997.

Then his wife Janet Jagan became Prime Minister for two years between 1997 and 1999, rounding off the tale rather nicely. A classic anachronism if ever there was one! A White American woman in charge of an Afro-Guyanese and East Indian community that had struggled so determinedly for their own cultural identity.

Yet the Guyanese have been unable to shake free of the strictures of race. To this day, voting largely remains based on racial background. In the main, the P.P.P. usually attract the Asian-Guyanese vote, while the P.N.C. attract the support of the Afro-Guyanese.

Although G H Mathieson's novel may have been spoof fiction, some of his predictions did materialise. Under Cheddi Jagan's influence, a complete immediate break with the Colonial powers could well have bankrupted the economy, and left with little equipment and infrastructure to share by means of their socialist ideals. Under Burnham's handling, perhaps the country simply exchanged one Colonial power for another with Communist principles.

Despite the country having a stock of natural resources, its bauxite ores now only contribute 13% of their exports, and demand for timber is minimal. The world now requires a more renewable source of timber from coniferous forests. With the entrance of the UK into the European Common Market, demand for sugar cane was drastically reduced, because sugar beet became the more convenient alternative. Gold now accounts for the bulk of Guyana's exports, but that is hard-fought through a landscape decimated by a hit-or-miss destructive dredging process.

It was strange paradox. The country turned full circle, with socialite Jagan outliving his rival and led the country without controversy and without becoming radically Socialist. A peaceful revolution after all, and a Great Republic!

George Musgrave wrote the novel assuming that Communist ideology was being thundered around the country. Perhaps he, too, was taken in by fake news. But maybe, also, he played his small part in stemming a tragic demise.

Herein lies a dichotomy for an insignificant minnow of a nation trying to steer a course in a world of superpowers. While the desire is for self-reliance; that only comes with dependence and co-operation with others – a global partnership. George Musgrave was aware of this in his own vocation working among the people of Guiana. In the words of the hymn writer whose name he borrowed for the writing of this book:

Make me a captive,
And then I shall be free;
Force me to render up my sword,
And I shall conqueror be.
I sink in life's alarms
When by myself I stand;
Imprison me within Thine arms,
And strong shall be my hand.

George Matheson (1842-1906)

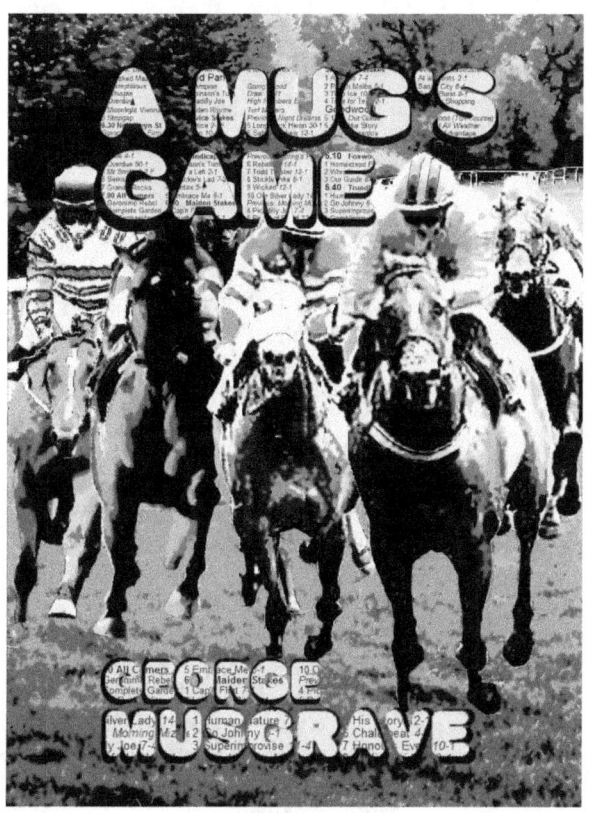

A MUG'S GAME by George Musgrave.

Roderick '*Infallible*' Fairman has stumbled on a way to beat the racing pundits using a dead-cert formula. The only trouble is, both he and his wife disapprove of gambling.
With thugs from the racing fraternity out to get his comeuppance, and the police and the Home Secretary concerned about falling tax revenues, he is forced to go on the run with his glamorous secretary.
Will he be caught before he brings the horseracing industry and the country to its knees?

Also by George Musgrave

Toward the Sunrise

We Journey On

The Great Republic

Friendly Refuge
(A Study of St Paul's Shipwreck and his stay in Malta)

Surprise

Paul and Thekla
(A Love Story of the First Century)

Martin My Son

A Speck of Dust
(The Story of George Musgrave)

What Happened to Anderida?
(In Search of Roman Eastbourne)

The following by George Musgrave are Edited by Andrew Musgrave:

Press on Brave Hearts
The Collected Poems of George Musgrave (1915-2012)

The Journeys of St Paul
from the Paintings of George Musgrave

The Dad I Never Knew

A Mug's Game

The Great Republic
(written as GH Mathieson)

Also by Andrew Musgrave

Fun Runs and Guns
(Trips and Trails through Yemen and Saudi Arabia)

Samak Fishing in Yemen

Orby:
How the spider lost its wings and learnt to spin a web instead

Penny, (the Vengeful & Sweet-Toothed) Sprite of Pen-y-Ghent

School Anarchy

Night Dreams

Children in Films

Children in Films is also published as eight separate volumes:

1 Gender Roles and Themes
2 Families, Step Kids and Orphans
3 Tomboys, Adventurers and Talented Kids
4 Childhood Friendships: Peers, Pets and Grown-ups
5 Make-Believe, Horror and the Supernatural
6 Puberty and First Love
7 Childhood Trauma: Illness, Death, Divorce & War
8 Physical and Sexual Abuse

Ambling Along Pennine Paths:

1 Lothersdale
2 Crummackdale and Austwick
3 Malham
4 Wuthering Heights and Haworth
5 Pen-y-Ghent

Rambling Through Lakeland Landscapes:

1 Rusland Heights
2 Stickle Pike & Broughton in Furness
3 Great Burney & Blawith Knott
4 Cathedral Cave, Little Langdale

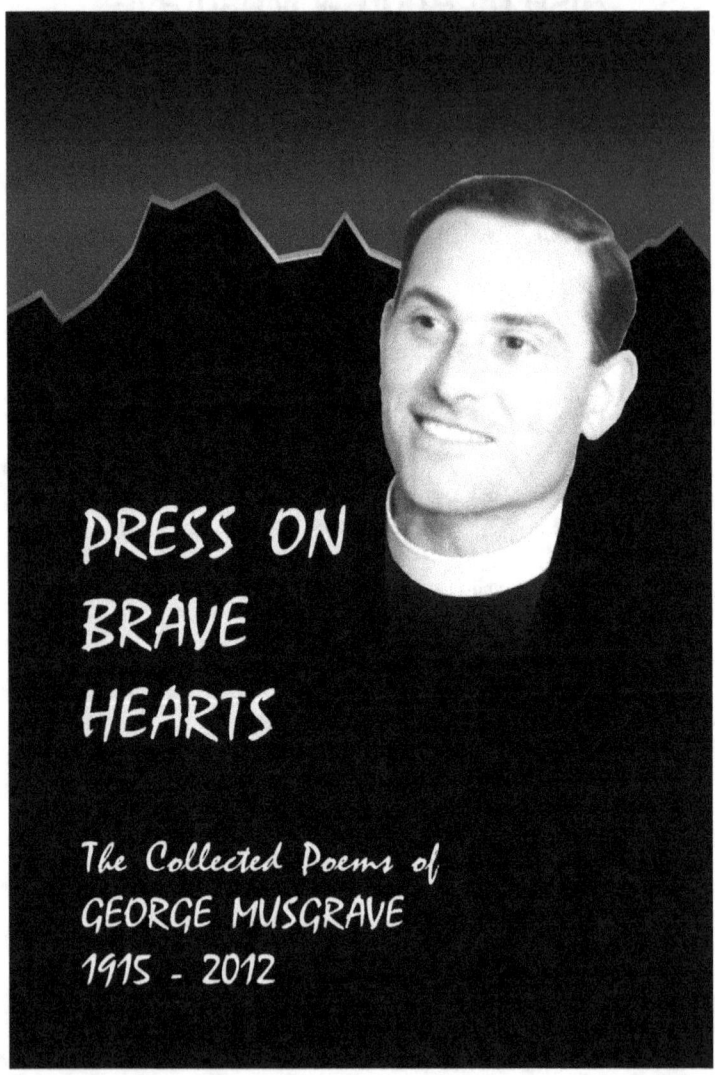

PRESS ON
BRAVE
HEARTS

The Collected Poems of
GEORGE MUSGRAVE
1915 - 2012

Press on Brave Hearts

George Musgrave died in November 2012, aged 97. He was a poet, an artist, a clergyman working among the deprived of London and British Guiana, a politician, a family man, an inspirer.

Taking his poetic writing (both secular and religious) from his youth up to his dying day, this book contemplates a lifetime of joy and love, reflects on the loneliness of rejection and of dying in old age, and the value he placed on prayer and faith.

"As we delve into the mystery of his verses, we open a Pandora's Box of intrigue and controversy concerning the romance of youthful days, of daydreams, of schoolboy pranks, of feelings of failure, as well as exhortations and resolve to succeed."

George Musgrave became a young man during World War Two while training for the clergy, and with a father killed on the battlefield of northern France, he had more reason than many to contemplate on the inadequacy of war as a solution to the problems of mankind. This is reflected in this compilation of all his poetic works, from the secular to the supernal, from rantings against the injustice of war, to the romance and confusion of an idealistic young man.

Some of his religious poems have been sung as hymns in various churches across the United Kingdom.

– acutely moving, – edifyingly inspirational, – deeply devotional.

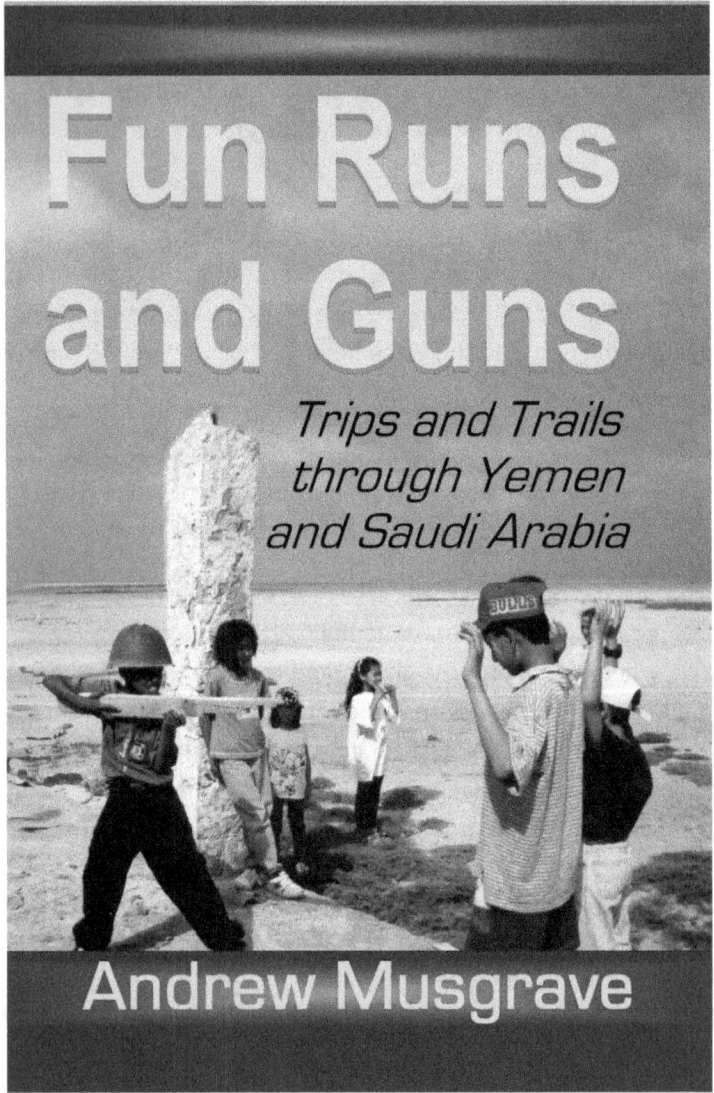